Four Square Miles

the layoff

Four Square Miles

A story of pride, love, family, and a dream.

KEITH MICHAEL PRESTON

ISBN: 978-1-7345925-0-4

Cover Art Designed by Thomas J. Zaffo/B. DeAngelo

Typesetting & Layout by Monte Press Inc.

Printed in the U.S.A.

I am forever grateful to my spouse, Nancy Preston, my mother, Diane Preston, and father, George Preston for their continued support.

I would like to show appreciation to the following individuals for their invaluable advice and ongoing support while creating this book: Caroline Adams, Annette Nasti-Coppola, Marie Miserendino, and Amy Corcoran.

FOUR SQUARE MILES is a series that takes place in a suburb of New York City.

the layoff is the first of the series.

CHAPTER 1

It's a crisp forty degrees on this October morning. Sun rays peek through vibrant red, yellow, and orange trees that surround an old sports park located on a fenced in corner of a bustling street. The large field within this sports park has seen better days. The grass is overgrown and weeds are sprouting through cracks on concrete paths where spectators once strolled.

Although this park is a depressing sight by all measures, and a local could become upset by even peeking at it, a man still intently gazes toward it while leaning on a rusty fence. He's wearing a gold sports jacket with black pants and his salt and pepper hair is combed neatly to one side. Even though his face is clean shaven, his battle scars reveal he's been around the block a few times. He is maybe five-foot ten at best, but his stocky frame fills out his jacket nicely, giving him a much larger appearance.

On one side of this dingy field, is a row of run-down bleachers that have given way to rats, other rodents, and possibly some squatters. Although it appears an absolute mess to the naked eye, the structure and setting help make it appear to be a place that could have been a spectacular sports park in the past.

In fact, up until a few years ago, it was, before it became an abandoned piece of property. Located on the south-east side of the city and directly across the street from a major parkway's exit and entrance ramps, it could be a dream location for something grand.

For a person who has vision and could imagine something for what it could be and not what it currently is, a large condominium development or a modern sports and entertainment venue could find a happy home here.

Nuccio "Nutsy" Gento just recently celebrated his fiftieth birthday. He grew up and still lives in this urban, inner-city located approximately a half hour north of Manhattan and just outside the Bronx, New York. The fact that it's a city in a world of its own and densely populated, helps give him a captive audience and is probably a major reason why he is so successful in his line of work.

As he stares in thought, Nutsy remembers spending many days playing baseball on this field in his youth. From time to time, he visits early in the morning and does the same thing, just quietly stares. Apparently, he has his own personal dreams and secrets about this place and won't share it with anyone, not even his family or close friends. Some speculate it could be just a childhood memory he rehashes or maybe, a grand master plan for the future.

Nutsy has been and is like a fixture in this city. He's well-known, feared, and possibly hated by some. It just depends on who you ask. But there's one thing that's certain, he now controls every sports bet that gets placed in this city. Right now, football season is in full swing with baseball playoffs just starting, so he's extremely busy and piles of cash are rolling in.

As Nutsy gazes toward the field with thoughts of what could be or what has already been, his sister, Blackie, approaches. She's a stunning beauty with an athletic shape, thanks to many years of dedicated black belt training. Her jet-black hair and customary black leather pants has helped her earn the nickname that suits her so well. Although she's much calmer now than in her younger years, she still carries a reputation around town of being someone you definitely do not want to mess with, period.

Blackie has seen Nutsy do this many times and always wonders what the hell he could be thinking about. The whole complex is a piece of crap and there's not much to imagine here even for the most creative person.

Nutsy turns as Blackie approaches him and says, "Maybe in my next life, Blackie."

The first thing that goes through Blackie's mind is, it's the same routine every time, so she replies, "It would be nice if one day someone knew what you're actually talking about."

Nutsy laughs and heads toward the street. "Come on, it's all a pipe dream anyway. I've got a busy morning."

Blackie follows and replies, "Hey, Walt had a dream one day, didn't he?"

As they both approach a parked, black BMW near the field, Blackie slides into the driver's seat and Nutsy into the passenger seat. She presses a button by the steering wheel and the engine roars to life. She always makes sure she has the twin turbo exhaust in her cars just for the thrill of the start.

Blackie presses on the gas and the car races down the street. "Loop by Turos. I wanna grab some crumb buns for the crew," Nutsy says while he slips out a four inch thick wad of cash from inside his sports jacket.

As Nutsy gets ready to count it, Blackie laughs and says, "Good luck counting that stash."

"Are ya kiddin' me? This is nothing."

Blackie's car races west across a busy, two lane avenue that cuts straight across the city with cars paralleled parked on each side. Depending on what part of the avenue you're currently on, you could be passing by houses or retail stores.

While Nutsy's hand flies through the bills like a counting machine at a bank, he has complete concentration since he has to get the amount right. After all, this is his livelihood and he needs to be certain by the time he's done, if this stack is short or not.

Nutsy wasn't the best student in his younger days, mainly because his mind always wandered during class. Although his teachers suggested he had a learning disability, they neglected to see that he was spectacular with numbers. He would spend most nights as a kid counting and studying addition and subtraction tables by himself. This was something he was always obsessed with even to this very day.

When he was a teenager, many of his so called friends didn't believe he could count so fast, so they would give him a mixed up stack of bills and wager he wouldn't get it right. Nutsy won all the bets except one, when a sneaky weasel cut a dollar bill in half before giving him a stack to count. It didn't take long for Nutsy to find out, but once he heard what the weasel did, Nutsy made sure he needed a few new teeth.

Once this news got around town, all the local bookies asked him to count their piles of cash to save them time. This was his beginning in the business and his purpose in life, but his principles have made him the man he is today.

Nutsy finally reaches the bottom of the stack and flicks the last bill. "They're fuckin' short again. When? When are these guys gonna get it right?" He shakes his head and stuffs the wad back inside his sports jacket.

Blackie is always amazed how fast his hands move through the pile and says, "I can't believe you can still count that fast."

"It's like riding a bike."

"Sure, maybe for you. I hate dealing with numbers."

"And ya work in a bank?"

"I was kind of forced to, remember?"

Nutsy laughs and replies, "I guess ya can say that."

As they now pass a park located on the left hand side of the street, Nutsy nods toward the park and says, "I remember mom sent me in there every morning on my way to school and said, "Nuccio, bring a dis onvelope to a da guy at dee a, bocce ball court. Capeesh?"

"You never told me that. How come?"

"That's where the old bookies had their coffee every morning."

"What was in the envelope?"

"Her numbers for the day. I never knew it until years later."

Blackie laughs. "She's a piece of work… so how's the group been going?"

Nutsy shrugs as they now approach a roundabout at a major intersection. "I've been fortunate, Blackie. These four square miles are still a blue-collar city. They all love to gamble… I can't say the same for the other guys. I heard they're all takin' a hit."

Blackie spins the wheel to curve through the roundabout and catches eyes with a young man looping behind her who rudely pumps his fist by his mouth toward her. It's early and Blackie thinks she should brush it off but decides to slam on the brakes anyway.

As her car skids and comes to an abrupt stop, Nutsy lunges forward and yells, "What the fuck!" While horns blare and echo down the street, cars swerve in various directions just missing one another. The roundabout is now at a complete standstill.

Blackie quickly leans her head out of the car window and says, "I hope that gesture wasn't toward me."

The young driver sarcastically replies, "Ya better believe it was!"

Nutsy has a feeling where this is heading and says, "Let's go. Hit the gas."

Blackie totally ignores Nutsy and slides out of the car. Nutsy yells out the window, "Let it be! It's too early for this crap!"

Blackie doesn't want to hear it, so she waves Nutsy off and continues toward this driver. If there's one thing that sets her off, it's an obscene gesture toward a female, especially her.

The twenty year old driver is a cocky, up and coming wannabe named Vito, a real derelict. As he watches Blackie approach his car, Vito sarcastically yells out the window, "Ya coming to give me a —"

Blackie looses her patience and yanks out a switchblade from her pants pocket. She skillfully twirls the blade through her fingers and decides it's time to teach this young punk a lesson. She presses the blade against Vito's cheek and says, "I'm sorry, what were you going to ask me?"

While horns continue to blare down the street, pedestrians curiously pause to watch the exchange. It's becoming a real scene this early in the morning.

So Vito says with his cocky tone, "You better back off. You're fucking with the wrong guy."

"That's funny because you're messing with the wrong lady... so what do we do now?"

"I guess you don't know who I am?"

"You look like a guy who enjoys fist pumping his mouth to females."

"Yeah, to the good looking ones."

Blackie presses the blade harder against his cheek and a spec of blood appears. "Take it out," she says.

"What?"

"Let's see what you got, tough guy. I bet it's no more than five inches."

Vito stares straight into Blackie's eyes for a moment. He can't figure out how this lady has the nerve to approach him like this so he replies, "My name's Vito. You better remember that."

"Don't worry, I'll remember."

Nutsy decides it's time to get out of the car. He has seen this many times growing up with Blackie, but this exchange is going on too long and he knows, the longer it goes on, the more dangerous Blackie can become.

Blackie laughs at Vito's comment and removes the blade from his cheek. "I'd like to say you're like all the other men, but you're still a punk kid." Blackie moves away from the car.

Vito's not finished being a smart-ass so he yells out his window, "Ya got a nice ass, ya know that?"

Blackie has heard enough from this young punk, so she leans over by the front of his car and stuffs the knife into a tire. The tire immediately goes flat and Vito leaps out of his car. "You bitch!"

Vito heads toward Blackie, but pauses when he sees Nutsy approaching with his hand inside his sports jacket. Nutsy stares Vito down and says, "It's time to take a walk."

Vito assumes that Nutsy is holding on to a pistol inside his jacket so he decides it's best to surrender, and with a smirk, slips back into the driver's seat.

Nutsy doesn't let himself get bogged down with petty bullshit anymore unless he truly has to. If this was twenty years ago, while Nutsy was making his mark, Vito would have wound up in the hospital. Nutsy's established and a family man now, so he doesn't need to press the issue any further with this young punk.

At this moment, Blackie slides back into her car and slams the door shut with a pissed off look on her face. Nutsy slides into the passenger seat and says, "Ya feel better now?"

"As a matter of fact, yes I do."

"Good. Drive me back home, I forgot to shave."

Blackie slams on the gas and the car peels out. "Do me a favor, stay the hell out of my business next time. I'm not fifteen anymore." Nutsy can't help but laugh. Blackie continues on, "It's not funny. This is all because of your crumb buns."

"Ya better hope your manager didn't see this."

"He can kiss my ass too."

While Nutsy laughs, Blackie heads into the roundabout and passes Vito who is now staring at his tire. "I hope you have a spare, Vito."

Blackie hits the gas and proceeds north up a small hill about a quarter of a mile and turns right onto a one way street. This street is like most streets in the city, made up of multi-family homes on small lots that take up the majority of the property, practically butting up to one another.

As they reach the middle of the block, Blackie pulls over in front of a stucco colonial style house that's nicely manicured with lush landscaping. Nutsy opens the car door and says, "I'll be awhile. I'll drive back myself. Thanks for the excitement this morning."

"Yeah, you're welcome. Just remember what I said."

Nutsy shuts the car door and moves away with a laugh. As he strolls down a blue-stone walkway toward his front door, the lawn sprinklers turn on. "Shit!"

While Blackie's car takes off, she yells out the window, "That's what you get."

CHAPTER 2

Nutsy enters his house with wet hair and his wife, Kathy, approaches him in the foyer and says, "Sprinklers again?"

"I gotta change the timer. I'm gettin' tired of this shit."

With her long blond hair and hypnotizing green eyes, Kathy is one of the most gorgeous women you will ever see. She's educated and street-smart, too.

Kathy was brought up by her father from the age of twelve after her mother had lost her battle with cancer. Her father was hesitant in the beginning when Kathy and Nutsy first met because of Nutsy's reputation around town, but he quickly realized Nutsy was an honorable and prideful young man and would never harm his daughter in a physical way.

To this day, he still wishes Nutsy was in a legal occupation, but he accepts him for the man he is. He does though, from time to time, attempt to convince Nutsy to get out and finally become legit.

Nutsy removes his sport coat and chucks it on a chair in the foyer. The house is tastefully decorated with cream colored walls that compliment oak wood floors. Custom base and picture frame moldings run across the bottom of the walls with chair rail in the middle. It's definitely an above average home in this modest neighborhood.

Kathy takes a glimpse at Nutsy's face and says, "It looks like you forgot to shave."

"Yeah, thanks," Nutsy replies as he climbs the oak wood tread staircase and removes his shirt. He roams into their custom bathroom with white Carrara counter tops and floor to ceiling imported Italian tile and chucks his shirt into a hamper. He spreads a handful of shaving cream across his face.

Kathy wanders down the hallway passing the bathroom and walks into their bedroom. It's not overdone, but someone with good taste could tell that the cherry wood furniture is very expensive. Kathy appears to be on the hunt again as she pauses to think, where is it?

She lifts a picture off of their bedroom wall and places it onto their bed. Her hand slides into an opening in the back of the picture and what do you know, she finds another one of his stashes.

From time to time, Kathy searches for these stashes for personal reasons of her own. She promised herself she would never be left without a large cash reserve again, like when Nutsy got hit for big money years back.

Nutsy eventually settled up on all his debts, but not without a real struggle for them both. Although she knows this money is tucked away, she wants to be one hundred percent sure it's stashed away for a rainy day and Nutsy will not blow it on the horses or Atlantic City.

Every once in a while, to scratch an itch, Nutsy would take trips to Atlantic City and blow a small fortune. The time they severely struggled still remains in the back of her mind and it's something Kathy will never feel comfortable about for as long as Nutsy remains involved with his sports business. The only thing that helps ease her mind is the group of surrounding bookies that Nutsy formed to help limit his risk.

Now Nutsy fights with a dull razor. He slides it down his cheek and flinches. "Fuck!" As blood trickles down the side of his face he yells, "Kathy!"

Kathy nervously places the picture back onto the bedroom wall. Of course, that was after taking half the stash. She strolls into the bathroom and notices Nutsy pressing a towel against his cheek. "I told you. You rush when you're shaving."

Nutsy chucks the razor onto the counter and says, "Just get the regular one next time. These fancy ones ain't worth shit."

"They were on sale."

"Ya know the old saying. Ya get what —"

Kathy cuts him off. "You pay for?" She's been hearing these lines forever.

"Well, it's true. Check those out." Nutsy nods toward the counter.

Kathy picks up tickets stubs and takes a peek as her eyes open wide. "No way! Front row to Maiden?"

"Yup, I promised ya front row one day, didn't I?"

Now Kathy excitedly hugs Nutsy like he's her best friend. In fact, they are best friends. They've known each other like a book since high school and challenge each other when need be. "How'd you get them?" Kathy curiously asks.

"Let's just say, they fell off —"

"The truck… your lines are getting old now."

Meanwhile, Nutsy presses the towel on his cheek and peeks down at her pants pocket which seems a little thicker than normal. Kathy notices and quickly turns.

"How about this new line, someone's been clipping my provolone. Ya know anything about that?"

Kathy lifts up a brush and strokes her long blond hair. She shrugs like, I don't know.

So Nutsy presses on, "We must have a mouse that's a thief then. Every time I look, the cheese is getting nibbled on."

"I guess it's hungry. Buy the Swiss next time, it might not like it." Kathy always has a comeback and is ready for Nutsy.

Living with him all these years has kept her on her toes. Or maybe, all the years living with her, kept Nutsy on HIS toes. So Kathy doesn't want to drag out this conversation any longer and says, "I have to run. I'm late." Kathy places the brush on the counter and gives Nutsy a peck on the cheek.

While Nutsy stays quiet and gives her a look, Kathy wanders out of the bathroom and says, "Don't forget, we have to meet the counselor later."

"I thought we went over this shit already?"

"Just make sure you're there on time, please."

Nutsy tosses the towel on the counter and replies, "It's a waste of time. She's been hanging out with her aunt too much."

As Kathy steps down the staircase, she pauses and yells out, "Thank you for the tickets!"

"Yeah sure, just make sure the mouse doesn't eat them too."

Kathy laughs and walks out the front door.

Nutsy strolls into the bedroom and opens a closet door. Suits, sports coats, and collared shirts are neatly lined up in a row. It's extremely organized with custom cabinetry. Nutsy slips on a new shirt and heads back downstairs.

He strolls through the kitchen with white cabinets and granite floors, and takes a seat at a marble island. He reaches into a jar and pulls out a stack of cookies and shoves them into a plastic bag.

CHAPTER 3

Nutsy steps out of his house and strolls back down the blue-stone walkway while keeping his eyes on the sprinkler heads just in case they pop up again. He heads toward his two-seater black Mercedes-Benz which is parked on the street and opens the driver's side door and slides in.

The inside is all black and the custom package makes it appear like a cockpit in a plane filled with buttons and devices. Nutsy presses a button on the dashboard and the engine roars. When he hits the gas, he presses another button on the dashboard and a classic rock station turns on.

He now approaches the roundabout and notices Vito leaning against his car with the tire still flat. Nutsy mumbles to himself, "This fuckin' moron probably doesn't even know how to change a tire."

Nutsy loops around the roundabout and heads south on a busy avenue toward the business district. It's a long street that runs north and south of the city, mainly with retail stores on each side. It's probably one of, if not, the busiest street in the city.

As his cell phone rings through the car's blue tooth, Nutsy presses a button on the steering wheel and answers, "Yeah?"

Ladro, Nutsy's right-hand man is on the other end. "Would you believe fucking Munchie doesn't have the vig?"

"And this guys a doctor? How much did he bet?"

"Five hundred straight and a five hundred teaser."

"Times or dollars?"

"Times."

Nutsy shakes his head and replies, "Are ya talkin' just the vig or what?"

"I think that's what I said, wasn't it? You have coffee yet?"

Nutsy laughs and replies, "Your wife screwed me all up this morning."

"I'm not gonna ask. What should I tell him?"

"Tell 'im to have the seven-fifty by next week, the latest. I'll see ya soon." Nutsy presses the button on the steering wheel and continues driving down the avenue.

It's about a minute later when Nutsy pulls over in front of Sista Bar and Grill that's conveniently located in the heart of the city. It occupies a two story brick building, well not exactly, because the bar is on the first floor and his sports operation is on the second.

Nutsy slides out of the car and closes the door. He strolls toward the entrance and before entering, exchanges hugs and handshakes with a few pedestrians. You would almost think he was the mayor of this city, but his tough appearance and voice would give it away.

He strolls inside the grill and eventually pauses by a square bar in the middle of the room surrounded by stools. The place is trendy with upscale décor scattered around as tables surround the perimeter and TVs cover the majority of walls with of course, sports games on.

A barmaid notices Nutsy and approaches him from behind the bar. As she bends over to pick up a baseball helmet off the floor, Nutsy catches a few young men sitting at the other end of the bar glancing at her rear. "Nutsy, did you leave this here last night?" She asks while placing the helmet on the counter.

Nutsy doesn't respond. He's too focused on these young men nudging each other while making gestures toward her. They finally catch Nutsy glancing at them and quickly turn away. He will never allow any of his workers to be disrespected, especially a woman. She doesn't know what's happening and asks again, "Nutsy, did you?"

"It's for your son. Tell 'im Santa came early this year," Nutsy replies as he moves toward the young men.

The barmaid shakes her head and replies, "You don't have to do this all the time, you know."

"I know."

As Nutsy makes his way toward the young men, they know he's coming and don't look his way. While he passes them, Nutsy says, "Let's be good today, gentlemen." They know that was a polite way of threatening them and they remain quiet.

Nutsy now continues toward a staircase in the back of the bar. He climbs the staircase and pauses by a door on top. While he bangs twice and the door quickly opens, Nutsy shakes his head and says, "I thought I said don't open the door, unless it's three knocks?"

Ladro, one of the ten thieves of Harlem years back, is standing by the door. They became great friends at a young age even though they traveled in different circles but always respected each other's territory.

When Ladro took a bullet in the leg during a botched job, it hindered his cat like performance, especially while climbing. Since Nutsy knew that Ladro's thieving career was now over, he decided to offer Ladro a position. They've been together ever since.

Ladro replies, "Your knocks are all the same anyway. You're getting predictable in your old age."

"You sound like my wife now." They both laugh as they exchange a handshake.

This is where it all happens and is known as, The Headquarters. There's a large conference table in the middle of the room covered with laptops. A nice size granite bar is on one side of the room and a pool table and couches on the other. Four large flat screen TVs are on a wall, each with sports games on. A fabulous feature is the TVs can act as four individual or one large screen. It's the kind of place you would never want to leave if you're an entertainer.

They both move toward the conference table and Nutsy asks, "What's movin' today?"

"They're gobbling up the teasers like they're cookies."

"Thanks for remindin' me."

As they both take a seat at the conference table, Nutsy pulls the plastic bag from his pocket and places it on the table. "I was gonna get crumb buns but your wife sidetracked me this morning. Ya gotta settle for chocolate chips."

"No oatmeal and raisins?"

"Over chocolate chips, ya gotta be nuts."

"Hey, I have to watch my figure."

Nutsy laughs and replies, "Ya never answered me from before."

"Giants, Rams, Packers are the heavy ones so far."

"Ya lay it off yet?"

"Talk about that. Squalo called earlier. He wants a meeting with the group."

"Great... let's see what the fuck the stooges want now."

CHAPTER 4

Kathy enters an office at a local bank where Blackie currently works. When Blackie was younger, she was mixed up with a local group called The Lincoln Lords. Her mother was beside herself and begged Nutsy daily to help get her out since they were involved with illegal activities. Although her mother knew what Nutsy was mixed up with, she couldn't comprehend her daughter being associated with a group like this.

After months of relentless battles between Nutsy and Blackie, Nutsy tried a different approach with one of his wife's ideas. He made a deal with Blackie and told her he would pay for her college if she left the group. It took a while with some brutal family arguments, but she finally decided THAT life wasn't for her anymore and took Nutsy up on his offer. Blackie would never admit it, but she does miss the action.

When Blackie finished college, Nutsy made a deal with the bank manager who owed him a ton of money at the time. Nutsy told him he would eat half of the vig that was owed him, if he gave Blackie a job. The funny thing is, Nutsy didn't have to eat the vig for the manager to agree, but he felt it was best to have the manger think he was doing him a favor.

Blackie glances up from her desk after hanging up from a phone call and asks, "You need the box?" Kathy nods while Blackie stands up and moves away. "Follow me." Kathy follows Blackie toward the back of the bank and they both enter a room with floor to ceiling safe deposit boxes.

Blackie slips a key into a slot and slides out a long, slim box. "Take your time. I'll be in my office." Blackie hands Kathy the box and walks away.

Kathy enters a small enclosed room and closes the door. She removes a pile of cash from her pants pocket and shoves it into the box. The box is already stuffed with cash so she has to push it down hard to pack it in tightly. Kathy flips the top over, which can barely close all the way now and leaves the room.

Kathy approaches Blackie in her office again and says, "This is full. Can you set up another box for me?"

Blackie replies, "Nutsy hasn't figured this out yet?"

"I think he has an idea, but I don't care. I need to protect myself if there's ever a next time." Kathy hands the box over to Blackie.

"But he has the group now, which he didn't have before."

"Yeah, sure. Like we can trust those guys."

"I know what you mean. Ladro isn't too crazy about them either."

"We'll talk later," Kathy says as she turns and walks out.

It's about three-thirty in the afternoon and Kathy and her daughter, Sammy, sit quietly in Sammy's high schools counselor's office impatiently waiting for Nutsy to arrive. Sammy is a tough, young lady and one could say she's almost following in her aunt's footsteps. Although Nutsy loves his sister and what she has become, he wishes a different path for his daughter, especially starting out in life.

Kathy notices the counselor, sitting behind the desk, getting antsy and was ready to apologize for her husband's tardiness as Nutsy suddenly races in. "Sorry I'm late. I got stuck in a meeting." Nutsy takes a seat next to Sammy.

The counselor smiles at Nutsy and replies, "Thank you for coming, Mr. Gento."

"Thank you for having me. What seems to be the issue here?"

"Well, I wanted to discuss your daughter's plans after high school with all of you."

"What plans? She's going to college, isn't she?"

Kathy has an annoyed look on her face. She can already tell where this conversation is heading.

The counselor peeks toward Sammy and waits for her to reply. "I already told you, dad. I'm enrolling in the Navy."

"What are ya talkin' about? We already discussed —"

Sammy cuts him off and replies, "No, you discussed it, not me. I'm eighteen and can make my own decisions now."

"Own decisions? You don't even pay one God damn bill at —"

Kathy can't keep quiet anymore. "Nutsy, watch your mouth!"

Nutsy stands up and approaches the counselor. He offers his hand and says, "Enroll her at a local college. I gotta go. It was a pleasure to meet you."

The counselor replies, "You also, Mr. Gento."

Nutsy races from the room and Kathy tells the counselor, "It's better that he's not here anyway."

"I heard that!" Nutsy yells from the hallway.

Kathy glances toward Sammy and says, "How about you try one semester and see how it goes?"

"I don't care, ma. You can enroll me, but I won't go to class."

The counselor replies, "It can never hurt to apply. You won't be bound by it and at least you will have other options by the time you graduate. You never know how you'll feel then."

Kathy senses what the counselor is attempting to accomplish and gratefully replies, "That's a great idea. The more options you have in life the better it is. What do you think, Sammy?"

Sammy stays silent and shrugs.

CHAPTER 5

Nutsy drives north on the B-R Parkway to meet his group in The Plains while listening to his standard classic rock station. The group is made up of four bookies from surrounding towns, including him. Years back, the group was specifically designed to spread out their bets and pocket the vig. The vig is the extra money, or let's say interest a loser pays their bookie besides the wager.

The first and oldest member is Squalo. He's sixty-five and extremely shifty, like a real shark. One will never know which direction he's heading in and he can turn on a dime. He also has the most experience and tremendous insight of the business out of the group.

Another member is Belo, who's fifty and a true gentleman, but can be easily swayed. Of them all, Belo and Nutsy have the best relationship since they were teammates on a baseball team years back. Belo earned his nickname because of his chiseled face and slim, model like body.

A third member is Donnola, a real conniver and weasel. He'll go along with anything Squalo says just to please him. He'll never admit it, but he's been jealous of the attention Nutsy always got since they were kids. It figures, Squalo and Donnola are best friends, a shark and a weasel.

Nutsy didn't initially want Donnola in the group but eventually agreed since his business was getting larger and needed additional outlets to lay off his bets. The ironic thing is, Donnola was the young punk who cut the bill in half and lost a few teeth by doing it, so there's already tension between the two of them.

Every week they call one another and try to lay off their bets with each other. If need be, it could be daily. What this means is, they try to balance their books with even bets. The idea is to have every game even and not guess the winner. All they care about is pocketing the vig and if they can balance their books, they're guaranteed winners for that week.

Everyone thinks being a bookie is about bettors losing their games. Maybe in the old days, but with the experienced ones today, it's about the guaranteed money with limited risk.

Nutsy parks his car in a metered parking lot and then strolls down a busy avenue passing new bars and restaurants that line the street. All he can think about is, shit, what a fuckin' gold mine here.

He opens a door to a building that's a high-end, high-rise and strolls through a large lobby. He eventually makes his way and pauses at a counter where a security guard peeks up from reading a book. "Hey, Nutsy, he's expecting you." They shake hands.

Nutsy replies, "How ya been?"

"Great, my daughter just celebrated her sixteenth birthday.

Where's the time going?"

"When ya figure it out, let me know." Nutsy pulls out a stack of bills from his pocket and sorts through it. He removes a hundred dollar bill and offers it to the officer. "Here, it's a gift from my family."

"It's alright, Nutsy. You don't have to —"

"I insist."

The security guard nods and accepts the money. "Thank you, Nutsy. Only you and Belo offered."

"That doesn't surprise me one bit with the other two. Enjoy your night."

Meanwhile, Belo and Donnola sit in Squalo's dining room with poker chips in front of them. A large, baby shark tank illuminates from a corner of the room.

After mixing a drink in his custom kitchen, Squalo wanders into the dining room and chucks something into the tank. "Watch 'em fight over this meatball, it's fucking great."

Belo's anxious to finish their prior conversation from earlier. It's a topic that's not currently sitting right with him. "Fuck them. Let's finish before Nutsy gets here."

Squalo replies while staring at the tank, "Listen, Belo... I can understand your concern, but things need to change and you know it."

"Hey, what can I say? We all control our own cities, but Nutsy's the one who lucked out with The Vern."

Squalo takes a seat at the table and shuffles a deck of cards. "Yeah, but between fantasy football and on-line gambling, WE'RE getting slaughtered, not Nutsy."

"Look, we all know The Vern's a close-knit city and still uses a bookie. That doesn't mean we have to try to purposely fuck him."

Donnola cuts in, "You're okay with his business growing and ours shrinking? Not me."

"What could we really do? Let's be serious here, he controls that city from top to bottom," Belo replies.

Squalo responds, "We go with the original plan. You're the split vote."

Donnola chimes in, "Yeah, he's just been using us all this time for his layoffs, so we'll use him now."

Belo knows he's now getting pushed into a corner. As he thinks it over, his mind drifts to an earlier time when he was standing at a bar with Nutsy during a fundraiser. A deeply connected Judge strolled over and shook Nutsy's hand and said, "Thank you for donating to my wife's charity."

Nutsy replied, "It's always my pleasure, Judge. Give her my best… this is my friend Belo. He's a good man."

Belo and the Judge exchanged a handshake. At that moment, Belo knew Nutsy was a deeply connected and respected man. Whether it was from the contributions or not, it didn't matter, he was well liked.

Squalo gets impatient while waiting for Belo's reply. "Well?

He's gonna be here any minute now."

Belo's not ready to commit. He also knows Nutsy donates new baseball uniforms to the Little League every year and takes care of the local cops during Christmas time. Squalo and Donnola are known to be incredibly stingy but Belo is torn since he's seen a dramatic decrease within his operation as well.

Belo finally replies, "Yeah, but you're forgetting, he's the main donor around here, not us."

Squalo says, "Let's be real here. He's getting too big on his own. One day he'll have us eating cat food from a can."

Belo replies, "I'm not sure if Nutsy would purposely do that. He's always been a stand-up guy."

Donnola cuts in, "Why, you wanna take that chance? Not me."

Squalo chimes in, "Well, as far as I'm concerned, if he doesn't take the deal, then we go with the other idea. Make him eat the whole fucking pie every week."

The weasel agrees. "Yeah, that's a better idea anyway. Then he'll beg us after he gets hit again."

Belo's not convinced yet. "So he keeps his own bets. We've all done that before."

Squalo replies, "Yeah, and look what happened to him years back. Why do you think this group was born?"

The doorbell rings and Squalo pushes for the vote. "Are we in agreement or what?" Donnola nods but Belo stays silent.

Squalo notices Belo's hesitation and presses on. "It's only, if he doesn't agree to the deal."

Belo stares at the fish tank in thought. He and Nutsy have always been cordial and friendly with each other. Belo knows it's not right what they are trying to accomplish but also knows what they are saying is correct, so he hesitantly agrees. "I don't see this going well, but I don't like cat food either. Don't get too close to him. That's all I'm saying."

Squalo replies, "The kid has calmed him down anyway."

"The kid?"

"Yeah. He hasn't had the same intensity for years."

"We're bringing the kid into this now?"

Donnola chimes in, "You can see it in his eyes. The kid has softened him up."

"That's right," Squalo says. "When was the last time Nusty took anyone down?"

Belo responds, "Even the fiercest lion in the jungle takes a rest."

"And that's when a poacher takes him down," Squalo sneers.

The doorbell rings again. Squalo stands up and struts toward the front door knowing he now has the majority vote. He did his job with them, but now has to get it passed Nutsy without any major issues. He knows this is not going to be an easy feat, especially if Nutsy feels cornered.

Squalo opens the door and Nutsy stands there impatiently.

"What are ya takin' a shit or something?"

Squalo laughs and gives Nutsy a hug. "Come on. The guys are inside already."

So they both move into the dining room and they all exchange a handshake. Although Nutsy notices everyone's quiet, he doesn't make anything of it and places a pile of cash onto the table. "I know it's early, but here's my contribution for the racetrack."

The four of them have been putting money away to buy into a deal that supposedly is coming up at a nearby racetrack. The racetrack is proposing to build a luxury hotel on their grounds and the group needs a million to buy in, so they've been placing money into their own private fund.

Squalo removes a picture off the wall and cranks a wall safe dial back and forth a few times. He turns a handle and yanks open the door. Piles of cash are inside. Squalo removes the money off the table and shoves it into the safe. "We're doing well. We got about six hundred and fifty seven after this."

Nutsy takes a look at the tank and asks, "We still need a mil for the buy in?"

Squalo slams the door shut and spins the dial. "Yeah, you have to see them eat this eggplant." Squalo chucks something else into the tank.

Nutsy replies, "Christmas Eve must be a feast with these things."

"Believe me. They know it's around the corner."

Nutsy takes a seat at the table and says, "It would be nice if someone other than Munchie knew the code, just in case you both croaked together."

Squalo replies, "Don't worry, there's a second in line."

Nutsy sarcastically replies, "Ya kidding? The way he's been gambling lately? Ya better start sleeping on this table." Nutsy peeks around the table and not one of the men cracks a smile. "Why do I feel like I'm not here to just stick more honey in the pot?"

The men glance back and forth toward each other waiting to see who's going to deliver the news. Squalo as always, takes the lead. "Alright… the way the industry is going, we all feel it's fair to split everything equally from now on."

Nutsy laughs and replies, "That's the best fuckin' joke I've heard in a long time." He glances around the table and no one still cracks a smile. In fact, only Squalo gives him a look while the other two glance down toward the table. Nutsy gets a feeling like something isn't right and stands up to put this comment to bed. "I don't think so. Vern pulls in over fifty percent of the revenue."

"Yeah but —"

"So ya want me to do fifty percent of the work for twenty five percent of the profit? This ain't a charity."

Donnola puts his two cents in. "It's only right."

Nutsy blows his top. "Only right! It's my donations that keep your ass outta fuckin' jail! Your pants don't even come with pockets."

Belo finally cracks a smile and Nutsy notices. "See? Belo knows."

Squalo now tries to push Nutsy into a corner. "Maybe so, but it's better than your nuts dangling again."

"And why would my nuts dangle?"

And here it comes from Squalo. "It's simple. If you don't agree to the split, we ain't taking your layoffs anymore."

Nutsy peeks back and forth at the men. They can't look him in the eye. He now knows he's getting pushed into a corner so he hesitantly says, "How do ya like this shit? The group I started is shaking ME down." He glances toward Belo and asks, "You're quiet, Belo. You're in too?"

Belo feels horribly about this but hesitantly nods yes. Nutsy shakes his head and continues on. "I gotta say, these two pricks don't surprise me but you, Belo, I'm disappointed in ya."

Donnola chimes in again. "You've had it too good for too long, Nutsy."

Nutsy moves closer to Donnola and says, "Ya nothin' but a fuckin' chipmunk!"

Donnola springs up. "Let's face it! You'd be shit without Blackie and the thief!"

As Donnola leans in closer toward Nutsy's face, Nutsy suddenly wraps his hand across Donnola's throat and yanks him toward the fish tank. "You're fuckin' going in now." Nutsy has incredible strength for his size.

Squalo and Belo spring up and race toward Nutsy. They both nervously attempt to separate Nutsy's hand from Donnola's throat, but Nutsy has a firm grip. After a struggle for a bit, they finally remove Nutsy's hand from Donnola's throat and Donnola gags while attempting to catch his breath.

Nutsy's now irate. Steam blows from his ears and the guys know it. He points toward Squalo and says, "And you, the fuckin' ring leader!"

Squalo cuts him off. "What's your damn answer?"

Nutsy hesitates while they stare at each other. "I'll think it over."

"You have till this weekend."

"In the meantime, I hope ya choke on the fuckin' chips." Nutsy violently swats his hand across the table and poker chips and baskets of appetizers fly through the air as he storms away.

Belo's thoughts were correct. "I knew it." He glances at Donnola. "I told you to stay away, didn't I?"

Donnola shrugs as Belo glances toward Squalo and says, "He seemed a little intense to me."

Squalo replies, "If this was years back, Donnola would be missing a few more teeth. Besides, don't worry about anything. If he doesn't agree, he will after this weekend."

CHAPTER 6

Half an hour later, Nutsy arrives home highly agitated. As he enters his foyer and chucks his jacket onto the same chair he usually does, Nutsy mumbles to himself, "I'll shove 'em all in that fuckin' tank next time."

He races into the living room, lifts up a gallon of red wine off a hutch and shakes his head. "Kathy!"

About a minute later, Kathy wanders into the living room. "What's wrong?"

"How many times do I tell ya, it's Paisano, not burgundy."

"They were out."

"This shit stains my teeth." Nutsy's dying for a drink after his meeting, so he pours a large glass anyway and chugs it.

Kathy senses something isn't right. "What's going on? You look uptight tonight."

Since Nutsy never discusses his business he replies, "Nothing."

At this moment, Sammy enters the living room and quickly turns around after noticing Nutsy's in the room. She's still annoyed from the meeting with the counselor. Nutsy notices and says, "Yeah, go ahead. Walk outta the room when ya see me."

Sammy turns back after deciding she needs to get something off of her chest. "Just so there are no surprises, I requested the Navy Seal application."

Nutsy sarcastically replies, "I hope ya enjoy sand up your ass."

Kathy can't keep quiet anymore. "How could you say that to her?"

Sammy replies, "You always tell me to follow my dreams, but now you are telling me not to."

"Just not that dream," Nusty responds.

"That's not fair," Sammy replies as she races out of the room.

Kathy isn't done yet. "You're a hypocrite. You know that?"

As Nutsy pours himself another glass of wine, he replies, "And why is that? Tell me, please. I'm dyin' to hear this."

Kathy sarcastically replies, "She needs to make her own decisions. How do you expect her to grow up?"

"Fuck this." Nutsy bolts out of the room and heads toward the front door.

"Where are you going?"

Nutsy opens the front door and replies, "To talk to my sister and put an end to this shit once and for all."

Nutsy walks out and slams the door closed.

CHAPTER 7

Nutsy now drives down a street a few blocks away from his house and pulls up in front of Blackie's brick style colonial. He gets out of his car and races up to the front door and bangs on it a few times. As Nutsy impatiently waits, the door finally opens and Ladro stands by the entrance. "What's up?"

"Where's Blackie?"

"She's downstairs hitting the bag. Come in."

"We gotta talk later. Don't go anywhere."

Nutsy races through the dining room and down the basement stairs. While Blackie pounds away on a heavy bag with rights and lefts, Nutsy races through the unfinished basement toward her.

Blackie notices Nutsy and pauses as she wipes the sweat off of her forehead with her forearm and removes her gloves. She's in phenomenal shape with stunning, toned legs. "My handsome brother. To what do I owe this late visit?"

They kiss on the cheek and Nutsy asks, "Are ya puttin' these Navy Seal ideas in Sammy's head?"

"Of course I'm not. Why do you ask?"

"Ya know she idolizes you."

"Nutsy, she's eighteen and a tough young lady."

"I don't give a shit if she's twenty-five and a world champion fighter."

Blackie laughs and replies, "How fast you forget. We were both on the streets at thirteen... come on, let's go upstairs."

They both move through the basement and head toward the staircase. "That was different. Dad died and we had to support mom."

Nutsy follows Blackie up the staircase and into the kitchen. While Nutsy takes a seat at a black and gold swirl granite island, Blackie removes a water bottle from the refrigerator and asks, "You want one?"

"Nah, get me a scotch."

As a black puppy races over and places its front paws on Nutsy's leg, he reaches down to pet the puppy's head and asks, "When did you get 'im?"

"Her. Last week. Ladro, get Nutsy a scotch!"

"What's her name?"

"Would it be anything other than Bandit?"

"I guess not, with you two."

Blackie laughs and replies, "Look, Nutsy, she's a smart girl and knows what she wants in life. You should be happy and let her flap her wings."

"If she's so smart, she should go to college. No disrespect to the Seals, I love them, but I only have one daughter. I can't lose her too."

Blackie quickly stands up and cuts him off. "You didn't lose anyone, Nutsy. Don't you dare even go there!"

As Nutsy and Blackie stare at one another, Ladro strolls in and places a large glass of whiskey in front of Nutsy. "Here, it sounds like you need a full one."

Nutsy glances toward Blackie and says, "I gotta talk to Ladro for a minute."

"If you need me to crack some heads, you know where to find me... and trust your daughter's judgment." Blackie moves away. "Bandit, let's go!" Bandit races away.

Ladro takes a seat across from Nutsy at the island and says, "I heard all about it."

"How?"

"Belo reached out before and said to keep an eye on you, that you almost lost it tonight."

"I try to control my temper, but that fuckin' weasel sets me off." Nutsy gulps from the whiskey glass.

"I'm surprised at Belo. You two were the three and four batters for years."

"Listen, you've been with me from the start. What does your gut say?"

"Hey, our nicknames didn't come from nowhere, did they?"

"I know, but times are different. We're big now. One wrong week and we can kiss our houses goodbye."

"I say fuck them, Nutsy. It ain't our problem their people are swaying." Ladro was always a risk taker. That's what made him a fearless thief before he got shot.

"Yeah, but it's all about balancing the books today. We're guaranteed winners that way."

"We ain't accountants. We're street-guys with principles… in the end, it's all we got."

Nutsy knows Ladro is right but this is different. He's not the young man he once was when he took big risks. But he's never been the type to back down, especially if someone was purposely trying to screw him over.

CHAPTER 8

The next morning Kathy walks down a long hallway at city hall where she's worked for years as a secretary. As she turns a corner, she bumps into Munchie who is a prominent doctor and one of Nutsy's big players. Munchie is the one who has the code to the safe in Squalo's apartment in case something happened to him.

The group knows Munchie for years and figured it was best to use a person not associated with their business. The only reason Munchie agreed to it was because Nutsy had asked him and most people can't turn down a request from Nutsy even if they wanted to, not even a big time doctor.

So Kathy asks, "Hey, Munchie, what brings you here?"

"I'm trying to expand my office. I need a permit… what happened between your husband and Donolla last night?" Munchie always hears the news from one of them in the group considering they all use him as a doctor.

Kathy shrugs and replies, "I have no idea. Why do you ask?"

"Kathy!" As Blackie's voice echoes down the hallway, both Kathy and Munchie turn and notice her heading toward them. Munchie doesn't want to get into it in front of Blackie so he says, "We'll talk later."

While Munchie moves in the opposite direction of Blackie, Kathy waits until she approaches and nods her head to follow her into a room. They both enter a vacant room and Kathy asks, "Did your husband say anything about Nutsy last night?"

"No. Why?"

"I don't know. Munchie said something happened between him and Donolla."

Blackie peeks at her watch and replies, "What else is new with them two? I'm on lunch. What's up?"

"I can't talk to Nutsy about this. I don't know if I'm doing the right thing with Sammy."

"Stop worrying, will you. Between the both of you, you're going to drive yourselves nuts."

"This is different though… can you show her a few things, maybe it could help her?"

Blackie replies, "I would love to." A smile beams across Blackie's face.

Blackie couldn't wait to show Sammy a few moves, so she invited her over the next night. Sammy was thrilled that her aunt would take the time to work with her. She always wanted to ask, but just never got up the nerve since she always thought her father would get pissed off at her.

Sammy is the complete opposite of Blackie. She has blond hair like her mother but has a stocky frame like her father.

While in Blackie's basement in gym apparel, they both take turns pounding away at the heavy bag to warm up. Blackie's impressed with Sammy's strength and thinks she has raw, natural power. "Okay, now for a few moves. Let's line up and face each other," Blackie says.

As Blackie and Sammy square off toward each other with fists up in the air, Blackie nods and says, "Okay, now come at me, but hard. Try to take me down."

Sammy dances a little like she's in a boxing ring then quickly charges forward but Blackie side-steps, snatches her arm, flips her onto the mat, and kneels on her throat. All Sammy could think about while lying on the floor was, holy shit! She's like fucking lightning!

Blackie takes some pressure off of Sammy's throat and says, "Now, in a life or death situation, once you get them down, you have to finish them." Blackie throws a powerful right and smashes the mat right near Sammy's face. "You got that?"

Sammy nervously flinches and closes her eyes since she wasn't expecting that at all. Blackie wants to make sure Sammy totally understands what she is trying to say. "You can't be afraid. It's either you or them. It could be the difference between coming home or not… you try now."

Blackie hops up and offers her hand to Sammy and yanks her off the floor. They both square off toward each other again with fists up in the air. "Alright, now I'm coming after you. Are you ready?"

As Sammy nods, Blackie side steps and spins around with lightning speed. Sammy attempts to grab hold of Blackie's arm, but Blackie's already behind her with a choke hold.

So Blackie tightens her arms around Sammy's neck firmly just to prove a point and says, "Now, did you see what I did? To be effective, you must not give your moves away. Always make them think something different is coming." Blackie lets go of her grip.

Sammy turns and replies, "Wow, I can't believe how quick you are, Aunt Blackie."

"You'll get there. Let's get a drink of water and work on the fun stuff, kicks."

CHAPTER 9

While at the Headquarters, it's a busy night of action. Sports games are on the TVs and a few customers are shooting pool with cash spread out around the edges of the table. Nutsy would let a select group of people come upstairs and play every once in a while. Of course, he takes a percentage of the pots and charges double for the drinks. No one cares though, since they think it's a privilege to be asked to participate.

While a few men and women tend to phone calls at the conference table, Ladro, like most nights, is busy handling calls himself since Nutsy always wants Ladro to be the lead person.

A phone rings nearby Ladro and he answers, "Sista!"

Munchie is on the other end and replies, "Munchie for Ladro." That's the code he's getting ready to call in a bet.

Ladro grabs a pen off the table and says, "Go ahead, Munchie."

"Forty times on the Vikings, and sixty on the Giants."

"Your cabbage is still past due, just in case you forgot." They always try to keep the conversations and information to a minimum and not mention dollars or cents at all.

"I didn't forget," Munchie replies.

Ladro jots on a pad and says, "What else?"

"Forty times, two game teaser, the Saints and Chargers."

Ladro taps a laptop keyboard and peeks at the screen. "Okay, that's Chargers plus four and Saints minus one."

"I thought the Saints would be even?"

Ladro replies, "You get six points on the two game teasers, right? Plus five minus six, is minus one, last time I checked MY arithmetic."

"Oh, I didn't realize the line on the Saints dropped to five."

"Yup… best of luck, Munchie." Ladro hangs up the phone. Go figure, they always tell the players at the end of the call, that they wish them the best of luck.

A two game teaser is a bet when the bettor has to pick two teams and gets to allocate six points to each team's spread. Both teams have to win in order to hit that bet. It appears easier with the six point allotment, but there's a reason it's called a teaser.

So Nutsy now strolls into the Headquarters and takes a seat at the conference table. Ladro glances toward him and says, "It's busier than Grand Central tonight."

Nutsy nods and remains quiet. Ladro knows him like a book and that this decision is playing on Nutsy's mind. "Let's roll the dice, Nutsy. Trust me. These fucking people couldn't pick an orange off an orange tree."

Nutsy cracks a smile and replies, "That's a keeper."

At this moment, Blackie wanders in and overhears Ladro. "Roll what dice?"

Ladro attempts to play it off and replies, "Atlantic City. Where do you think?"

Blackie is not a fool and gives Ladro a look like, yeah right.

As Ladro attempts to laugh it off, he stands up but flinches while grabbing his leg.

Blackie notices and says, "You know you can't sit too long. It stiffens up."

"Yeah, just like my third leg," Ladro sarcastically replies.

"Try more like, two and a half." Blackie will take any opportunity to bust his horns.

Nutsy laughs and replies, "I gotta say, there was no better cat burglar back then. Ya should've been a gymnast or somethin' like that."

Ladro replies, "Who knows, maybe he'll strike again with all this bullshit going on."

"Blackie interjects, "What bullshit?"

Nutsy quickly replies, "Nothing, he's just fuckin' around."

Blackie glances back and forth to both of them. She's not buying it at all.

Meanwhile, when Kathy gets out early from work the following day, she decides to roam around the house searching for more piles of cash. She removes the same picture off of the bedroom wall that usually has cash stuffed behind it. Not this time. Either Nutsy moved it or spent it, so she places the picture back onto the wall and stares in thought. A door closes downstairs so her search for tonight is over.

The next day during lunch, Kathy decides to take a trip back home and search some more. She has a gut feeling that something is brewing because of the remarks she hears from Munchie and Blackie and it's making her feel uneasy.

This time she decides to search around the kitchen, so she opens a drawer, feels around, and closes it. She pauses for a moment in thought, then moves toward a closet door and opens it. This was an area she never thought of searching until now. It's your typical pantry closet packed with boxes and canned foods.

So Kathy removes a cereal box and shoves her hand in it. Since there's no cash in it, she places the box back onto a shelf and removes another box. While she feels around in the next box, she smiles and whispers, "Sure, you like Captain." She slides out a large stack of bills, splits the stack in half and shoves the rest back into the box.

Nutsy forgot something at the house so he enters the front door and closes it. Kathy hears the door close and nervously shoves the bills into her pocket and places the box back onto the shelf. She quickly moves to the island and pretends to read through some mail.

Nutsy wanders into the kitchen and Kathy asks while she glances at an envelope, "What are you doing home so early?"

Nutsy notices that Kathy appears a little edgy and replies, "What are YOU doing home so early?" Nutsy peeks toward the closet and notices that the door is still open. "Listen, I'm not gonna tell ya again. Stay away from my cheese. A lot of things are going on now."

At this time, Sammy and a young man walk into the kitchen and Sammy says, "Great, you're home."

Regardless of their relationship, Kathy will never let Sammy disrespect Nutsy, especially in front of guests. "YOU'RE is your father, in case you forgot."

And of course Nutsy has to get his point across. "Yeah, I only pay for the toilet paper ya get to wipe your ass with."

Kathy shakes her head and wonders, why does he always have to stir the pot? "Who's your friend?" Kathy asks.

"It's Bono," Sammy replies.

Bono, like a true gentleman, offers his hand to Kathy. "It's nice to meet you, Mrs. Gento."

Kathy shakes Bono's hand and replies, "Likewise."

Bono offers his hand to Nutsy. "And you, sir. It's a pleasure." Bono has been respectful so far and that is probably the only reason Nutsy hasn't tossed him on the street already.

Nutsy hesitantly shakes Bono's hand and replies, "Take a walk with me."

Sammy flips out. "He's doing it again, ma!"

Kathy's not thrilled with this either. "Is this really necessary?"

"We'll be right back." Nutsy glances toward Bono and says, "Follow me." So Bono follows Nutsy out of the kitchen.

Sammy's says, "He does this all the time. I'm sick of it."

Meanwhile, Nutsy's ready to drill Bono in the back of the living room. "We're ya from, Bono?"

Bono remains calm and replies, "The Hills, sir."

"Ya go to school?"

"I'm a senior like Sammy is."

"Are ya going to college?"

"I'm not going to college. I joined the Army."

Nutsy stares at Bono for a moment and thinks this young man is at least respectful. He remembers the first time he walked into Kathy's house when they had first met and her father was hesitant of his reputation, but gave him a shot because he was respectful.

Bono senses Nutsy's hesitation and wants to ease his mind. "If you're concerned about me and your daughter, we're only friends, sir."

"There's no such thing as a friend at eighteen... if ya get my drift?"

"I'm gay."

"You're what?" Nutsy is caught off-guard.

"I don't date girls. Sammy and I are just friends."

Meanwhile, Sammy stews while she paces back and forth in the kitchen. "I'm not going to miss this house at all."

Kathy tries to reason with Sammy and replies, "He's only watching out for you. One day you'll understand."

As Nutsy and Bono both stroll back into the kitchen, Nutsy glances toward Sammy and says, "Stay outta trouble. I gotta nuff shit going on right now."

Sammy doesn't acknowledge him. In fact, she turns in the opposite direction just to prove a point and says to Bono, "Let's go!"

Bono still remains calm and respectful and says, "It was a pleasure meeting you both."

While Sammy storms out of the kitchen, Bono takes his time to not seem disrespectful. Kathy shakes her head and says to Nutsy, "And you wonder why she wants to join the Navy. To get away from you!"

"Just leave my provolone alone."

As Kathy storms out of the kitchen, she gives Nutsy a look and replies, "Tell your mouse friend that!"

CHAPTER 10

Later that afternoon, Nutsy waits in one of Munchie's examining rooms looking to square up on a few bets. It's a typical ten by ten waiting room with an examination table and chair. While Nutsy sits on the chair scrolling through his phone, Ladro wanders in and closes the door.

Nutsy still scrolls on his phone and says, "These phones are ruining the world. Ya know that?"

"You're not shitting," Ladro replies as he takes a seat on the edge of the examination table.

"Ya can't hide today with these things, it's like everyone's up your ass... you can give me a quarter and a pay phone any day of the week."

Ladro laughs and replies, "Pay phone? You sound like a dinosaur, right now."

"Trust me, I'm feeling like one."

Munchie enters the room and closes the door behind him. Nutsy stands up and says, "Here he is, the man who can't pick his ass with his middle finger."

Munchie laughs and replies, "Tell me about it. I'm like the kiss of death right now." Munchie gives Nutsy a hug.

Ladro replies, "That's just wonderful. Our doctor is the kiss of death."

They all laugh as Munchie slides a stack of bills from his pocket and plops it into Nutsy's hand. It's a pretty thick stack so Nutsy wants to make sure the amount is correct and begins to count.

As Nutsy's fingers fly through the stack as usual, Ladro and Munchie both watch in amazement. It's almost hypnotizing watching Nutsy count a stack of bills and it doesn't matter if the bills are in order or upside down, he still gets it right. So Nutsy flips the last bill over and says, "You're off two-forty."

"How do you figure that?" Munchie replies.

"Ya did a forty time teaser, right?"

"Yeah, but the Saints won by five. I pushed on that bet."

Ladro replies, "Are you playing games now? There ain't pushes with teasers."

Munchie digs into his pocket and replies, "Oh sorry, I never pushed on a teaser before."

So now Munchie nervously flicks through his roll of cash and places another stack of bills into Nutsy's hand. Nutsy takes a quick peek since it's a much smaller amount and shoves the bills into his pants pocket. Now that Munchie is fully paid up, Nutsy changes the conversation and says, "So who do ya think's gonna be the next captain?"

Munchie replies, "It has to be the big guy."

Ladro says, "Without a doubt."

Nutsy replies, "Yeah… some future he has, huh?"

"That's for sure. I like him, a real class act," Munchie says as he lifts a blood pressure sleeve off of a small counter. "Let's at least make this visit official. I'll check your blood pressure."

"Yeah, just don't surprise me with a fuckin' bill at the end of the month."

So Nutsy rolls up his sleeve and Munchie wraps the blood pressure device around Nutsy's bicep and pumps a few times.

Besides stopping here for his cash, Nutsy thinks now is a perfect time to ask Munchie about another thing that's been on his mind lately. "Let me ask ya something. Who does Squalo have down to give the code to, if something happened to him?"

While Munchie listens through a stethoscope, he attempts to avoid the question and replies, "I don't know how you do it. It's always perfect."

"Ya just need two things, Munchie, red wine and a lot of garlic."

As Munchie and Ladro both laugh, Nutsy hasn't forgotten his original question so he makes sure Munchie knows exactly where he's coming from. "I got a lot of hard-earned money in that safe, ya know."

Munchie hesitates but knows he can't avoid the question so he replies, "I heard what's happening. I promised Squalo I'd only give it out, if something happened to him."

Nutsy stares Munchie straight in the eyes and says, "Fair enough. I'm only asking ya, who's second in line?"

At this moment, Nutsy has the standard look on his face when he wants something like you're going to give me the answer to my question one way or another. Munchie has seen this look many times from Nutsy growing up and knows if he doesn't give him a satisfying answer, this scene could become ugly, and quickly.

Munchie nervously peeks toward Ladro who gives him a shrug like, don't look at me for help. So Munchie finally nods and says, "It was you but he changed it to Belo recently. Please don't say anything."

Nutsy smiles and gives Munchie a hug. "Ya know I won't. We'll talk later."

As Ladro hops off the examination table, he flinches while grabbing his leg. Munchie notices and says, "You need to go back to physical therapy."

"I need a lot of things, Doc, but I'll take lasting more than five minutes these days."

Nutsy shakes his head and replies, "That's just what I wanna fuckin' hear."

Ladro laughs and says to Munchie, "Don't tell anyone it's acting up. I gotta keep up my reputation."

Nutsy sarcastically says, "Yeah sure. Maybe, we should change your name to gimp… let's go before he asks to stick his finger up our ass."

CHAPTER 11

Later that evening at the Headquarters, Ladro and a few men sit on a couch gazing toward the big screen TV. They're watching a playoff baseball game on all four screens as one. It's like watching a TV that practically takes up the entire wall.

All of a sudden, Ladro chucks a donut at the screen and yells, "Take him out already! Jesus Christ… he's getting hit all over the park!"

As Nutsy approaches the couch, a man places a stack of bills into his hand. Ladro's still wound up and yells, "A hundred and ten pitches and they're banging him all over the place. Yank him you fucking moron!"

While Nutsy moves behind the bar and starts to count the stack of bills, he laughs and replies, "It's the same story every year with this team anyway." Nutsy places the last bill down on the bar and shakes his head. "You're short again."

The man who gave Nutsy the cash shrugs and replies, "How?"

Now Nutsy's a little annoyed. He and Ladro have explained how the system works over and over, so he decides it's time to lay it in. "How many times we gotta go over this? Each time is worth five dollars and a teaser vig is a hundred percent of the times."

"Sorry, I get the vig mixed up all the time."

"Ya better learn it because that's your pay. Now you get shorted."

Ladro takes every opportunity he can to bust balls. "Did you take math in school? If each time is worth five dollars, what's a hundred time bet?"

The man replies, "Five hundred."

Ladro continues, "Good. Now what's the vig on a straight bet?"

"Fifty."

"You see, it ain't rocket science here. Now if they lose a hundred time teaser, you're gonna collect the five hundred plus what?"

"… a hundred?"

"Look at this! You just graduated Gambling 101. Now don't fuck it up again."

The man embarrassingly shrugs while the other men laugh.

Nutsy has enough of explaining it over and over. "Fuck this. I'm gonna make a change that you'll understand. The vig is now called, the whack."

The man replies, "The whack?"

"Yeah, because if ya don't get it right next time, you're gonna get whacked in the fuckin' head."

As Ladro and the other men burst out laughing, he decides it's a good time to break some news to Nutsy that he might not care for. "Nutsy, you ain't gonna like this, but I think Blackie found out what's happening."

"How?"

"Who knows, probably at the bank or some shit like that."

Later that evening, Munchie's in his bedroom and slides up a pair of pants over his underwear. As a rough looking woman in a robe quickly moves away from the bed, Munchie asks, "Are you sure your father doesn't know about us?"

From the bathroom, the woman replies with a gruff voice, "Yup… and I want to keep it that way."

"What about the fix you said he was talking about?"

"I overheard him mentioning a game being a lock under."

"Do you know which one?"

"I think he said the Bears Packers. What does that mean anyway?"

"That means you take the under on the spread."

"What under?"

"Didn't your father ever explain this to you?"

"No, I was never interested in sports."

"It's the total points on the game. It means the score's going to be low."

"I hear you talking about teasers all the time. Is this something you would tease?"

"No, you'd take a straight under-bet and bet the house."

The same evening, Nutsy and Ladro sit at the island in Nutsy's kitchen discussing business over a few glasses of whiskey. Since Ladro's mind is always roaming, he's usually the first to come up with different ideas. "You wanna shave a point off the teasers? Maybe go to five on the two games and nine on the three games?"

"I don't know. We can't be the only ones doing it."

While Nutsy and Ladro discuss different business options in the kitchen, Kathy and Blackie sit in the living room with their own concerns after hearing the news about Nutsy's predicament with his group. "I don't like this at all, Blackie."

"Has he said anything to you?"

"Not a thing. What about Ladro?"

"Nothing. He'll never say anything unless Nutsy's okay with it. Let's not assume the worst yet."

"I have to. You know your brother. He'll never give into those three, especially Donnola."

Meanwhile, back in the kitchen, Nutsy has a different idea. "Maybe we'll charge full whack on every bet, not just teasers."

Ladro laughs and replies, "I gotta say, that's some funny shit about the whack."

"Is it me, or does this younger generation not get math? I mean come on, this ain't calculus."

Kathy, listening intently to their comments in the kitchen, tells Blackie, "There's no way I can go through this again. It took years to rebound."

"Yeah, but you're assuming he's going to get hit again."

"You know in that business it's bound to happen sooner or later."

"At least you're putting away money this time."

"Trust me. It's not enough yet and I have other concerns."

"What?"

"I just hope this doesn't affect N-J at all."

"Why would it?"

"The place's he's at is crazy expensive."

"I can understand that. What else?"

"It's been very quiet for a while and Nutsy's been good. I just hope he's not like a volcano waiting to erupt."

As Nutsy and Ladro stroll into the living room, Blackie quickly changes the subject. "Front row to Maiden and you couldn't get us tickets?"

Ladro loves Maiden. "No fucking way!"

Nutsy replies, "I didn't wanna see my sister in her black leather outfit all night." They all laugh.

Blackie replies, "Believe me, I'll never fit in that thing anymore."

Ladro says, "Remember we saw them in the eighties? I think my fucking ears are still ringing from that night."

Blackie shakes her head. "Do you have to curse all night?"

While Ladro shrugs, Nutsy's cell phone rings and he takes a peek. "What the fuck does this guy want now?"

Blackie shakes her head and says, "Both of you with this cursing."

"Who is it?" Kathy asks.

"Munchie."

"Munchie? Why is he calling so late?"

"Who the fuck knows," Nutsy answers the phone and asks, "Am I dying?"

Munchie responds on the other end, "Are you kidding me? You'll outlast all of us."

"What's up, doc?"

"Are you still taking action on the Bears Packers this weekend?"

"Of course, why wouldn't I?"

"Wow, I'm surprised."

"Surprised at what?"

"You're still taking action on that game, even though it's apparently a lock under."

"What lock under?"

Munchie hesitates while answering. "Oh, I thought you knew about it."

"This ain't the nineties, Munchie. No such thing as a lock anymore." As Nutsy gives Ladro a concerned look, both Kathy and Blackie notice.

"If you hear anything else, let me know," Munchie replies.

"Yeah, I'm gonna tell ya how to bet the spread."

"With all the money I've paid over the years, it would be a nice gift from you."

"I might be generous, but I don't wear a red hat and have a white beard."

Munchie laughs and replies, "We'll talk later."

Although he's been kidding around with Munchie, Nutsy hangs up the phone with a concerned look on his face. If Munchie is correct, this news could be devastating if Nutsy doesn't accept the deal. He seriously glances toward Ladro and says, "We better make some calls downtown tomorrow."

Kathy and Blackie catch eyes knowing this news can't be good by the tone in Nutsy's voice.

CHAPTER 12

The next morning, Squalo, Belo, and Donnola meet at a diner in New Row on Main Street. It's the same one they all used to go to at four in the morning after hitting the night clubs years back. It still looks exactly the same, maybe some updates here and there, but overall, it still looks the same.

Squalo orders his usual Broccoli omelet. Donnola orders a B-L-T, and Belo, still a health freak, orders oatmeal with raisins. It's the same thing Nutsy eats every morning. When Nutsy and Belo played baseball together when they were younger, they would meet at random diners and order the same food.

While Belo shoves a pile of oatmeal into his mouth, he mumbles, "Anyone hear about this lock coming up?"

Donnola replies, "It's all everyone in this town talks about."

Squalo smirks like a cocky son-of-a-bitch. Donnola notices and asks, "You knew it all along, didn't you?"

Squalo grins and nods. He always likes to surprise everyone with his shifty ways and gets a kick out of it.

Donnola laughs and continues on, "The shark strikes again… the only problem is, how do we lay it off, if we're all taking in the same bets?"

Squalo has already been toying with this scenario and replies, "If he doesn't agree, we'll push our bets onto Nutsy."

Belo replies, "How?"

"If anyone calls us for that bet, we'll tell them our shop is closed and they have to place it with him."

Donnola replies, "That won't work. Nutsy doesn't take any bets from people without an established account."

Like always, Squalo has a solution. "True, but everyone in our town has at least one friend in The Vern. They can use their codes."

Donnola comes up with his own idea. "How about we put pressure on Munchie? He's a big player in Nutsy's city."

Although Belo hesitantly agreed to the profit split in the beginning, he surely doesn't like how things are progressing. "I don't know about this idea of plotting behind Nutsy's back like this. It's not —"

Squalo cuts him off mid-sentence. "Why, because you two played baseball together years back? That teammate shit was another life ago. This is your fucking livelihood we're talking about right now."

Later that day at the Headquarters, Nutsy was anxious to make phone calls to some of his close downtown New York City associates. While he sits at the conference table on the phone with a bookie from the Bronx, Nutsy asks, "Are ya sure about this under bet?"

"About as sure as my hair falling down the fuckin' drain these days."

"If I need an outlet, are ya available for some layoffs this weekend?"

"I though you already formed a group up there in the sticks?"

"I did, but we currently have a difference of opinions."

"I see. This is a tough weekend to mess around… I'm sorry, Nutsy, I gotta pass this time but I'd be happy to discuss it after this weekend, if you'd like."

"Sure, if I'm not buried already."

"We might all be taking it hard this weekend. On a different note, next time you're around down here, give me a call. I'd love to treat you and your wife to dinner at my new restaurant on Arthur Avenue."

"Ya opened up a restaurant?"

"Yeah, it's fuckin' beautiful. You'd love it. My chef makes the best Eggplant Rollatini."

"Good for you."

"With the online gambling, our gig's not gonna last forever, Nutsy. We gotta start venturing out a little."

"I hear ya. I'll take ya up on it one day."

"Don't forget, best of luck with your search."

Nutsy hangs up and says to Ladro, "Everyone's sayin' the same shit. There's a lock coming up. Would ya believe this?"

Ladro sits at the bar and replies, "In this day and age, I'm still not buying it… will he at least take some layoffs from us?"

"Nope… they're all shitting in their pants right now."

"How about we just say fuck it, and cross that game off the list?"

"Nah… our credibility would go down the drain then." Nutsy picks up the phone and dials. "Hopefully, Manhattan might be willing to take some." The phone rings a few times and Nutsy impatiently waits for someone to answer.

A man with a deep voice finally answers, "Look who it is, my old friend, Nutsy. To what do I owe this pleasure?"

"It's been a long time, pal… I'm calling about this lock coming up."

"Yeah, make sure you protect yourself good and do whatever you gotta do. You know what happened last time."

"If I need to lay off some bets, are ya available?"

"Shit, Nutsy, you know I love you, but no one's taking layoffs on this game."

"No one downtown at all?"

"It's like asking an insurance company to insure you when a flood's coming."

"I guess so."

"By the way, how's Billy been?"

"He's away at some island right now chasing all the ladies."

The man laughs and replies, "Yeah, we both had some good times together years back. Last time we spoke, he mentioned about some secret dream of yours."

"It's only a dream, pal. Maybe, it will happen in my next life."

"Hey, you never know. You're still fairly young. Maybe after this weekend it might be time to finally chase it and get out. If so, give me a call. I'd love to hear about it."

CHAPTER 13

The following night, Sammy and Bono decide to hit a sports tavern on the west side of town. Sammy and Bono are having a great time laughing it up while standing by the bar. The bartender knows who Sammy is, so she slips them drinks here and there but makes sure they're in soda cans to not draw any attention.

Vito is also at the bar and has already been pounding down drinks for hours. His boss owns the bar so it's easy for the members to get cocktails. The one thing his boss doesn't go for, is anyone of her members getting out of line. She likes to keep the bar business and her underground business separate.

From the other side of the bar, Vito peeks over toward Sammy and Bono. Vito knows Bono from The Hills area where they are both originally from.

Sammy takes a sip out of her soda can and says, "I can't wait to start my Seal —"

At this moment, Vito approaches them and blurts out, "We don't allow fags in this bar."

Sammy turns, trying to figure out who the comment was directed at, and notices Vito glaring at Bono. "You can't talk to him like —"

Since Bono already knows Vito's reputation, he cuts her off to avoid any issues. "Sammy, it's alright. We'll just leave."

While Sammy and Vito lock eyes, Vito has the same cocky look he always has and sarcastically says, "How about you come back later and I'll show you a good time?" He turns toward Bono. "Now get the fuck outta here."

Bono doesn't reply since he knows he's no match for Vito, especially with all of Vito's friends around. He just wants to leave because he can tell Vito's drunk, which makes him even more aggressive than he normally is.

When Bono latches onto Sammy's arm and attempts to pull her away, Sammy resists while staring at Vito. She's not ready to bow down yet, especially because of Vito's cocky, sarcastic tone.

Vito sarcastically yells out, "I gotta better idea. How about we have a contest to see who sucks a better…" Vito now pumps his fist a few times by his mouth making the same obscene gesture he always does toward ladies.

Sammy has heard enough of his bullshit. She breaks loose from Bono's grip and violently throws a hard right striking Vito directly on his cheek which makes him stumble backwards. As Vito rubs his cheek and tries to gain his bearings, he stares at Sammy with an irate look on his face.

Vito now decides to charge at Sammy, but she sidesteps, grabs hold of Vito's arm, and flips him over. As he crashes onto the ground, Sammy quickly places her boot onto Vito's throat and presses down firmly. "Say you're sorry."

Bono can't believe what's happening and watches with his eyes wide open in complete shock. Vito doesn't want to give in so he remains silent without apologizing. As Sammy becomes impatient and presses her boot down harder, Vito gags and blurts out, "Ya dead, bitch."

A crowd surrounds them, which makes Bono even more nervous than he already is. In fact, he's shitting in his pants right now. Sammy doesn't seem to care and is not letting up until she gets some satisfaction. A man's voice yells out from the crowd, "Yo, dude, say you're sorry."

As Sammy becomes even more impatient and annoyed, she presses harder waiting for Vito's apology. Bono just watches in shock. He can't believe this is actually happening. Since Vito senses he's on his own without any help from the crowd, he hesitantly says, "I'm sorry."

Although it's not exactly the apology she was looking for, Sammy is content and removes her boot from Vito's throat and then races out of the bar with Bono.

The man with the voice, just another local derelict, helps Vito off the ground. Vito shakes his head an asks, "Bro, why didn't ya back me up?"

"You know who that is?"

While Vito rubs his throat, he shakes his head no. The man says, "That's Nutsy's daughter. You fucking idiot."

A few laughs echo from the other end of the bar and another man's voice yells out, "And this guy's a Lord? What a fucking chump."

Vito appears extremely embarrassed and pissed off at the same time. He knows this doesn't look good for his reputation, especially on his own turf.

Sammy and Bono race toward their car which is parked down the street from the bar. Bono still can't believe what he had just witnessed and says, "Sammy, why did you —"

Sammy's blood still boils and cuts him off. "He has no right talking to me or you that way!"

"He's a Lord though."

"I don't give a shit what he is. They're all idiots anyway."

"Still —"

"You can let them control your life, not mine."

It's now around three in the morning and Blackie and Ladro are both sound asleep in their bedroom. While Blackie's cell phone rings, which startles her, she quickly leans up and fumbles around the end table searching for it since its pitch black in the room. She finally finds it and rudely answers, "Whoever this is, better be —"

The lady with the same rough voice that was in Munchie's bedroom is on the other end. "It's me. We have an issue."

Blackie recognizes the voice and replies, "What's wrong?"

"Come to my shop first thing in the morning."

Blackie tries to go back to sleep but tosses and turns the rest of the morning. At about five-thirty, she decides to get out of bed and get ready since the lady who called is usually in her shop by six. Blackie didn't want to waste any time and was anxious to find out what the issue was. This can't be any good, she thought, since the lady called so early in the morning.

Blackie pulls up in front of a Body Shop in an industrial site and quickly slides out of her car and races into the store. A young secretary sits at a counter and notices Blackie charging in. "She's expecting you in the back."

Blackie nods and races toward the back of the lobby and pushes open a door. The lady who called Blackie in the middle of the night sits behind a large mahogany desk. Her name is Belinda and she currently runs the Lincoln Lords. Go figure, a doctor and a lady who owns a body shop and runs an illegal operation, are a couple. They say opposites attract, well they surely do in this case.

Since Belinda knows Blackie flies off the handle quickly from their dealings in the past, she attempts to start off the conversation in a diplomatic way and calmly says, "Have a seat."

"I'm good. What is it?"

Although Belinda tries her best to keep Blackie calm, she has her own reputation around town that she has to maintain for business and says, "I'm giving you the courtesy of —"

Blackie doesn't have any patience for the kindness right now. "I asked you, what is it?"

Belinda hesitantly replies, "Your niece fucked up one of my guys at my bar."

"Did he deserve it?"

"That's not the point. You were a Lord back in the day and know the protocol."

Blackie paces the floor and eventually replies, "Belinda, I swear on my mother, if she gets touched, I'll take you all —"

Belinda cuts her off before the conversation gets out of hand. "Let's not get —"

Blackie continues. "Just hope my brother doesn't find out about this. He'll flush all your punks down the toilet."

Belinda knows she's right. The minute Nutsy finds out, he'll travel to the ends of the earth to protect his family, especially his daughter. So Belinda knows she's in a tight predicament but she also has to hold her ground. "Easy now... you've been out for a while. It's a new crop of kids. They're a lot more violent than —"

Blackie doesn't want to hear this bullshit. "Yeah, I can see that. One of your punks got his ass kicked by a girl."

"She's no different than the two of us. We both kicked a lot of ass back then."

While Blackie and Belinda stare for a minute, the door swings open and Vito struts in with his usual cocky manner and pauses when he sees Blackie. "What the fuck's she doing here?"

Belinda has a confused look on her face and replies, "You two know each other?"

Blackie replies, "This asshole's a Lord?"

"Who are ya calling an asshole?" As Vito moves in Blackie's direction, Blackie tugs up her pants by her thighs and gets in a fighting stance.

Belinda quickly leaps in between them and says, "Whoa, she's a black belt. Back the fuck up." Belinda gives Vito a shove backwards.

Blackie asks, "Is this the kid who got his ass kicked last night?"

"I got sucker punched and who ya calling a kid?"

Vito knows Blackie's a woman and can't help but think how tough could she really be, so he decides to move toward her again. This time, Belinda grabs his arm and bends it forcefully behind his back. "What did I say?"

As Blackie and Belinda catch eyes, Blackie seriously says, "I'm expecting you to do the right thing before my brother finds out… and teach your punk some manners before I do." Blackie races out of the room and slams the door shut.

As Belinda lets go of Vito's arm, he quickly turns with an annoyed look and asks, "You take her side over mine?"

"I'm saving your ass, that's what I'm doing."

"How do you know that bitch?"

"That bitch is the aunt of the girl that just messed you up."

"We'll see about that one."

"You back off until I give the word. You understand?"

Vito struts away without acknowledging her.

Blackie, now livid, flies up a street heading north and passes every yellow and red light in her path. She yanks out her cell phone from her pants pocket and presses a button. While she impatiently waits for an answer, she floors the gas.

Sammy answers her cell phone while walking to school, "Hey, Aunt Blackie."

"Where are you?"

"Walking to school, why?"

"I'll be right there."

Blackie hangs up and tosses the cell phone on the passenger seat.

As Sammy casually wanders down the street, she begins to wonder why her aunt was so short with her on the phone. That was kind of strange, she thought.

It's a few minutes later when Blackie's car charges down the street and skids right on the side of Sammy. "Get in!" Blackie yells out of the passenger window.

Although Sammy's puzzled by her aunt's behavior, she doesn't question her and gets into the car. As Sammy pulls on the door to close it, Blackie slams on the gas and the door slams shut almost taking her arm off.

Sammy knows something's not right and peeks toward Blackie who stares straight toward the road without acknowledging her. Who pissed in her cereal this morning, Sammy wonders?

A few minutes later, Blackie decides it's time to hear Sammy's story. "So tell me what happened?"

Sammy still has no idea what Blackie is pissed off about and replies, "Tell you about what?"

"Last night." Blackie gives Sammy a look.

Sammy now knows what this is all about and attempts to play it down. "Ah, it was nothing, Aunt Blackie. It was just some local guy who was drunk causing problems."

"Don't play games with me. I'm not getting phone calls at three in the morning for nothing, am I?"

"Who called you?"

"That's none of your concern. Now tell me."

Sammy knows she has to come clean since she can tell there is no way her aunt is letting this go. "What was I supposed to do? He called my friend Bono a fag and asked us who sucks a better —"

Blackie cuts her off. "I got it… that derelict is one of the Lords though. You can't —"

Sammy is just like her aunt and doesn't like to back down. "I don't care who or what he is, Aunt Blackie. He has no right talking to me like that."

"You have to learn how to walk away at times."

"Would you have when you were my age?"

"That was different. I had —"

Sammy took this opportunity to prove her aunt wrong. "I heard what you did at the circle."

Blackie pulls over on the side of the road and slams on the brakes. She knows where Sammy is going with this, but she can't let her have the satisfaction. "I'm your aunt. Don't ever throw shit in my face again… just stay away and keep your mouth shut."

"But —"

"Do you hear me? I'm not teaching you how to defend yourself so you can rough up these local punks."

Sammy knows she hit a button, so she remains silent with an annoyed look.

CHAPTER 14

The following morning, Nutsy lies in bed wide awake while staring at the ceiling. His mind has been roaming over the last few days and it has been keeping him up through the night. As he rolls over onto his side, he peeks at the alarm clock displaying 3:45AM and shakes his head.

Finally, after dozing on and off for the next couple of hours, Nutsy decides to get out of bed. He drags himself into the kitchen and pulls the coffee maker out of a closet and fills it with water. He looks like a complete wreck with messy hair and dark bags under his eyes. As the coffee brews, he plops onto a stool by the island and impatiently waits for it to be done. "Fuck it," Nutsy says as he pours himself a cup without it being fully brewed.

It's about an hour later and Nutsy has finished the whole pot of coffee but he decides to make another full pot. While waiting for the coffee to brew, Nutsy pulls a picture out of his pocket and gazes at it with the same blank stare he always has while looking it.

As he glances at this picture deep in thought, Nutsy hears footsteps coming from the other room and quickly stuffs it back into his pocket.

Kathy eventually strolls into the kitchen dressed for work and notices Nutsy at the island. "You got up early." She peeks toward the brewing coffee. "You're just making coffee now?"

"It's a second pot. I already finished the first one."

Kathy texts something on her phone and then shoves the phone into her purse. "I have to run. I have a meeting in the office."

Nutsy nods while glancing at a newspaper and doesn't even look up to acknowledge her. Kathy knows something hasn't been right with him lately and says, "It looks like you slept on the wrong side of the bed."

Nutsy nods and replies, "I'd be happy with the wrong side right now." He flips a page of the newspaper without making eye contact.

"You need to learn how to relax."

"I'll relax plenty when I'm in the box. Don't worry."

"I'm sure you won't then either."

Kathy never confronted him about the news of his group and has no idea of his thoughts or decision. She always tries to stay out of his business but this is different. She already struggled with Nutsy being on his own with no support after he got hit for big money, and because of that, she wants him to take the secure way and not leave the group. So she decides to take this opportunity to start off a conversation and hopefully tell him how she feels. "Maybe, you're nervous about something?"

Nutsy's in no mood for small talk right now. "What are ya insinuating?"

Kathy stares for a moment wondering if this is really the time she should press on. She can tell Nutsy didn't sleep well and would be easily agitated. This has been eating away at her for some time now and she needs to get her point across so she decides to continue and replies, "I'm telling you now, you better accept the deal."

Nutsy replies while still glancing at his newspaper, "What deal?"

"Don't play coy with me. You know exactly what I'm talking about." Kathy's tone gets a little louder. She knows Nutsy is playing games now.

Nutsy peeks up from the newspaper and asks, "Ya buttin' in my business now?"

That's it. Kathy can't contain herself anymore. The stress has been building for too long. "Your fucking business! The last time you got hit, we were in a basement apartment with no heat for years!"

"What are ya talking about? There was heat."

"Yeah what, it barely hit sixty during the winter."

"Whatever."

"You better pray this doesn't interfere with N-J. It's expensive there and he's happy."

The house phone rings, which breaks the tension a bit. Kathy moves toward the counter and says, "I'd rather see you take a chance with this crazy dream of yours, whatever the hell it is, than throw your career down the drain." Kathy picks up the phone and answers, "Hello."

On the other end of the phone, at an exotic beach front resort, is her father. His real name is William and they all call him Billy for short. He is seventy-five years old and is in tremendous physical shape and has extremely deep connections. He's a very sharp-minded and sophisticated man. In a way, he helped Nutsy become the man he is today by introducing him to very influential people around the city, mainly politicians.

Billy replies while sitting on a beach, "I just got your text. Is he there?"

"Yeah."

"Put him on."

"I'll see you when you get back. Love you." Kathy hands off the phone to Nutsy. "It's my father. I'm going." Kathy walks out of the kitchen.

Nutsy has a feeling this isn't good so he hesitates before answering while trying to gather his thoughts. Billy wouldn't call this early in the morning for nothing, and, if it was that important, Kathy would already know about it. Nutsy finally answers, "Billy, why ya calling on your vacation?"

"Nuccio, your fingers break?"

"What?"

"I heard what's going on."

Nutsy stands up and paces around the kitchen. "I didn't wanna bother ya while you were chasing the young girls around the island." Nutsy laughs figuring he would throw Billy off.

Not Billy, he's a serious man when he has to be. "Never mind that shit… you gotta take this deal."

"How'd ya find out?"

"It doesn't matter, does it?"

"Ladro thinks —"

Billy cuts him off. "Look, I love Ladro, but he'd rather have his feet dangle in the air."

Nutsy becomes a little heated and replies, "And what, let these guys just jam it in my ass?"

"You're not thirty. You get hit again, you won't have the time to recuperate… besides, did you forget what we discussed already?"

Nutsy hesitantly replies, "Nah, I didn't."

"I keep telling you, going legal is the big picture, Nuccio, but you never listen… you screw up now and it will never be an option for you."

"Let's be real here, dad. What are the chances of that really happening? Even if I do this, there are no guarantees."

Billy has enough of the back and forth. "Nothing is ever guaranteed, Nuccio. If your aunt had balls, she would've been your uncle. Just take the safe way and get it fucking over with!" Billy hangs up the phone.

Kathy decides to stop by the bank before heading to town hall. She enters Blackie's office and waits for Blackie to hang up from a phone call. It's a minute later and Blackie finally hangs up and says, "I got the new box set up. Follow me."

Kathy follows Blackie into the safe deposit room. Blackie has been toying with letting Kathy know about Sammy's situation. Blackie would like to straighten it out before anything further happens, but she now decides it's only right that at least Kathy knows. "I have to talk to you about Sammy." Blackie slides the slim box out of the slot and hands it off to Kathy.

"About what?" Kathy asks.

Blackie hesitates and replies, "She roughed up one of the Lincoln Lords the other night."

Kathy sighs and shakes her head. "What am I going to do with this girl? Between her and her father, they're both driving me insane."

"I told Belinda to back —"

Kathy's eyes open wide and she cuts Blackie off. "Belinda?"

"Yeah, she's in charge now."

"This is just wonderful, Squalo's daughter."

"Just keep your eyes open. Don't tell Nutsy yet. I'm trying to take care of it before a war starts."

Kathy's cell phone rings and she answers, "Yeah?"

Nutsy's on the other end steaming after his conversation with Billy. "Ya called your father?"

"Called him about what?"

"I guess a birdie flew from New York to the islands then."

Kathy decides it's time for her to play coy with Nutsy now. "Why would a birdie do that?"

"Or maybe a crab told him while building sandcastles... just stay outta my business."

"You better do the right thing then." Kathy peeks at her phone. "I have to go." Kathy presses a button on her phone and asks, "How did it go, dad?"

Billy strolls on the beach and says, "Have you been putting money away?"

"I'm trying, but he keeps on moving the stashes around."

Billy replies, "Try harder. Knowing him, you're probably gonna need it one day."

CHAPTER 15

Later in the afternoon, Nutsy and Ladro stroll down a busy street on the northern part of town. Nutsy's still a little annoyed from the exchange with Kathy and says, "She's busting my balls now."

Ladro replies, "She's nervous, what do you expect?"

"And her father thinks we should take the deal."

"Well that, we could've bet on."

Nutsy opens the door to a tavern and they both step inside. As they both move toward a table in the back of the room, Ladro notices Squalo and Donnola seated at another table and says, "What the hell are they doing here?"

Nutsy replies, "Ah, who gives a shit? I'll be right back." While Nutsy heads in the opposite direction of Squalo, Ladro takes a seat at the table.

Squalo peeks over in Ladro's direction and whispers to Donnola, "The thief concerns me. Years back he cleaned out Harlem like a fucking Hoover vacuum."

"Don't worry. The shot he took in the leg will never let him climb again."

Squalo peeks back toward Ladro. "Yeah, never say never... look at him. He looks like a washed up thief licking his chops, right now."

Nutsy strolls back toward his table and catches eyes with Donnola. What an asshole, Nutsy thinks.

Vito struts through the front entrance and gives Nutsy a look while passing by. As Nutsy takes a seat at the table, Ladro notices the look on Vito's face and says, "Did you see the way that punk looked over here?"

Nutsy doesn't give a shit about Vito at this moment. He's the last thing on his mind. "Don't worry. He knows his place."

Squalo notices Vito's stare and asks Donnola, "Is that the new kid that works for my daughter?"

"How am I supposed to know? This isn't my city," Donnola replies.

As Squalo watches Vito strut away, he has a look as if he's scheming something like he always does. "You see that look he gave Nutsy?"

"No."

So now Ladro peeks over toward Squalo and Donnola and says, "Look at these two stooges... how much is in that safe anyway?"

"I don't know... maybe six-seven."

"What, thousand?"

"Yeah sure, try hundreds of thousands."

"Are you pulling my chain?" Ladro's eyes excitedly open wide since he never knew how much was actually in the safe.

"Look at you. Ya look like a kid who just got cotton candy at a baseball game." They both laugh.

Ladro still has the safe on his mind and replies, "You give me the word and I won't leave a piece of dust in that fucking thing."

Squalo decides it's time to say hello to Nutsy and Ladro, so he wanders over in their direction. It's not that Squalo really gives a shit about being cordial to them, he's been anxious to find out if Nutsy made a final decision or not.

So Squalo approaches their table in a calm manner and says, "Gentlemen." Nutsy and Ladro both exchange a handshake with Squalo. Regardless of their issues, a handshake is a must while saying hello.

"What brings ya down to this part of the world?" Nutsy asks.

"I'm meeting my daughter for lunch. We gotta discuss a few things."

"Yeah, I heard she's rising up around town."

"You can say that... have you come to any decision yet?"

Squalo just killed the conversation. Although Nutsy has an idea which way he's leaning, he's not ready to commit one way or another and of course, has to break balls now. "A decision about what, the layoff or the lock ya failed to tell me about?"

Squalo knows that was a back-handed slap and just stares for a moment. He can tell Nutsy isn't the calm, cool guy he usually is. "Have you been sleeping alright? Your eyes look a little puffy this morning."

Nutsy has enough of the bullshit. "What's your concern with how I fuckin' sleep?"

"To be honest, I really couldn't give two shits. Just make sure we have your decision by Saturday."

So Squalo strolls back to his table and takes a seat. "He's shitting in his pants. I can tell. He looks like a total wreck up close."

Vito struts back through the room and Squalo yells out in his direction, "Hey you, come here!"

Vito pauses and replies, "Who me?"

Squalo nods and Vito approaches their table and says, "What do ya want?"

Squalo replies, "You work for my daughter Belinda?"

"Oh, sorry, I didn't know you're Belinda's father."

Nutsy and Ladro both peek over wondering what Squalo's saying to Vito.

So Squalo says, "Take a seat for a minute."

As Vito takes a seat, Squalo asks, "Any of your friends in this town gamble?"

"They all gamble with that prick over there." Vito nods in Nutsy's direction. "Not me though."

Squalo and Donnola catch eyes. They can sense there's already tension between Nutsy and Vito.

Squalo is now ready to scheme and says, "I'll make a deal with you. You convince some of your friends to call in bets for me this weekend, and I'll give you the pick of the century."

"If it helps screw that asshole, I'm in. I don't care about the pick."

"You gotta keep this quiet though… and my daughter can't find out about this, you got me?"

As Vito nods in agreement, Squalo continues his conniving, "We'll see how you handle this. I might have some more projects for you, if I'm satisfied." While Squalo and Vito shake hands, Squalo catches eyes with Nutsy and gives him a smirk.

CHAPTER 16

Later that evening, Sammy and Bono sit in her living room having a conversation. Bono's fidgety since neither Nutsy nor Kathy are currently home and asks, "Are you sure it's okay, I'm in the house right now?"

"Yeah, as long as we're in the living room or kitchen... so how about the party I was telling you about?"

Bono glances at the front door. It's clear he is not comfortable being in the house at this time. "I don't know, Sammy. I'm not too thrilled about going in that bar anymore."

"It's a Halloween party. No one will know who we are with our costumes on."

Bono glances toward a picture on the end table that catches his attention. He picks it up and attempts to figure out what it is, but he can't make it out. "Why do you have a picture of an overgrown field?"

"I don't know. It's my fathers. What about the party, you didn't answer me?"

As Bono places the picture back down on the end table, the front door opens and Kathy walks in. Kathy notices Sammy in the living room and storms in with an annoyed look on her face. "Excuse us, Bono. I need to talk to Sammy privately."

Bono stands up and replies, "I have to get going anyway. It's nice to see you, Mrs. Gento."

Kathy nods while Bono moves away. Sammy still has the party on her mind. "Think about the party."

Bono nods and walks out the front door. Sammy glances toward Kathy and notices a stern look on her face.

It's about seven o'clock in the evening, and Nutsy and Ladro sit at the bar at Sista which is not too crowded. A few empty whiskey glasses are staggered in front of both of them already. They have been discussing different topics over many drinks. Nutsy is feeling good, but Ladro knows he hasn't been the same lately because he's been talking a lot about the past and what could have been. Maybe he has guilt, maybe some regrets, maybe, he is just not settled with life, Ladro thinks.

So Nutsy takes a sip out of a whiskey glass with a concerned look on his face and Ladro notices. "Nutsy, relax. We'll be okay. I know it."

Nutsy takes another sip of his drink and replies, "How much did we move last week?"

"Four-fifty."

Nutsy sighs and replies, "Four-fifty the wrong way and we'll be eating milk bones for decades." Nutsy takes another swig.

It all appears to be wearing on him and he changes the direction of the conversation. "Have ya ever thought about what your life would be like if ya followed your childhood dream?"

"I only had one dream. That was to hit a casino in Atlantic City or Vegas. It ain't happening with my leg now... I know you always wanted to be a baseball player."

"Yeah, it all ended when I left school to take care of my mother. I ain't complaining though, I would do it again, if I had to... how about as an adult? Ya have any other dreams?"

"Maybe, retire with Blackie on the Amalfi Coast one day... make wine and adopt a kid that we never had... I know you have a dream, but won't say."

"I can't. It was a wish when I blew out candles one year... I guess we can at least still chase 'em, ha?"

Ladro knows there is more to that comment than it seems. Nutsy and Kathy had to make a life altering decision about a year ago. "I know where you're going with this, Nutsy. We can't control —"

Nutsy cuts him off. "I know... it just ain't right though." Nutsy gulps his drink.

Ladro knows there is nothing he can say or do to sway Nutsy's mind, so he decides to lift up his glass in salute. "How about, to our adult dreams one day?"

Nutsy raises his glass and replies, "Now we just gotta figure out this mess first."

The barmaid approaches them from behind the bar. "Are you guys alright?"

Nutsy leans down and picks up a baseball bat and places it onto the counter. "It's the new composite. Your kid's gonna love it."

The barmaid shakes her head. "Nutsy, come on. I can't keep on —"

"You're only young once. Let 'im enjoy his time. I'll be right back." Nutsy stands up and moves away.

The barmaid glances at Ladro and says, "Ladro, I can't keep on taking all this from him."

"Just take it. It helps him out. Trust me on this."

The barmaid knows what Nutsy and Kathy had to do and knows where Ladro is coming from. "Okay. I get it."

So now Nutsy stands in a stall booth in the bathroom. He doesn't open his fly or pull his pants down, just stares in thought. Suddenly, he angrily pounds a wall with his fist. He pounds again and again like a boxer who had lost his control.

A few minutes later, Nutsy takes a seat next to Ladro at the bar. Ladro peeks at his wrist which is disfigured. "What the hell happened to you?"

"Nothing, I tripped."

"Let me see that?" Ladro takes a look. "Jesus Christ, Nutsy, I have to take you to the hospital."

"Ah fuck it. Let's just get another drink."

Ladro stands up. "Let's go. That thing looks broken."

CHAPTER 17

The next morning, Nutsy enters a building and walks down a hallway while holding a wrapped box with a soft cast around his wrist. It's a good thing Ladro took him to the hospital because it turns out, he has a hairline fracture.

Kathy was pissed off when she found out last night. Not that he had gotten hurt, but because of the excuse Nutsy gave her. He told Kathy he had tripped in the bathroom and landed on his hand the wrong way. It wasn't too hard for Kathy to figure it out, since Nutsy was still drunk when she arrived at the hospital.

Nutsy was a little annoyed at Ladro for even calling her, but Ladro had dinner plans already with Blackie and another couple.

As Nutsy continues down the hallway, a perky lady pops out from a doorway and says, "Hey, Nutsy."

Nutsy pauses and replies, "How's it going?"

"Good." She peeks at his hand. "What happened to you?"

"Ah, ya know. We're our own worst enemy at times."

"I guess so. He's in the back."

"Thanks. How's he doing?"

"Baseball playoffs just started. All he does is practice being a pitcher. You just missed Kathy."

"Ya have yourself a nice day." Nutsy smiles and continues toward a door.

He enters a room, and a young man, age twenty, is in the corner of the room winding up like a pitcher. The young man freezes and says, "Papa!" He races toward Nutsy and wraps his arms around him, tightly.

The young man is Nuccio Gento, Junior and they call him N-J for short. He has autism, and has been recently placed in this facility.

Nutsy and Kathy did everything within their power to keep him home, but N-J had grown into a strong young man and was beginning to put himself and others in physical danger. Although they were both in denial for months, they eventually decided it was time that N-J needed to be watched twenty-four hours a day. Nutsy wishes he took after Kathy's side of the family who are more mild-mannered than his side.

Everyone tries to convince Nutsy and Kathy it's in N-J's best interest to be in an environment that keeps him calm, but even so, it rips them both apart every single day.

Although Nutsy thinks his son was given a raw deal in life, he always tries to remain positive around his son since N-J can become easily agitated, like both Nutsy and Blackie do. The only difference, is N-J has no control over his temper whatsoever. There were times when he ran out of the house in the middle of the night and raced down the streets alone for no reason at all. He loves playing with knives too. That was their deciding factor.

"How's my boy doing?" Nutsy asks as they both move to a table and take a seat.

While Nutsy places the box on the table, N-J notices the cast on Nutsy's hand and asks, "What happened to you, Papa?"

"Ah, it's nothing, N-J. I just slipped in a bathroom."

"Oh." N-J can't keep his eyes off the cast. "Mama was just here."

"I know."

"Mama comes every day, but you haven't been lately."

"I know. I'm sorry. It's no excuse but Papa's been busy."

While N-J's eyes roam between Nutsy's cast and the dark bags under his eyes, Nutsy gets a feeling its troubling N-J and says, "Look at me."

N-J peeks up toward Nutsy, but his eyes continue to flicker back and forth. Nutsy knows something is bothering N-J and tries to calm his nerves. "N-J, look me in the eyes."

While N-J glances into Nutsy's eyes, he fights not peeking away, but he can notice the intensity in his father's eyes and remains focused on them. Nutsy now knows he has his son's attention and says, "Papa's alright. Trust me."

N-J replies, "Okay, I just want to make sure. You don't look the same to me."

Nutsy places his hand on top of N-J's hand and says, "You'd be the first person I would tell if something was wrong... right?"

As N-J smiles and nods, Nutsy knows he settled N-J's fears and changes the topic. "Your sister's graduating school soon. What do ya think about that?"

"I know, papa. I'm so proud of her... who's that box for?"

"Who do ya think?" Nutsy hands N-J the present. "Here, it's for you."

"That's for me?" N-J excitedly tears open the box and yanks out a baseball glove. "Wow, this is great! I love it! Maybe, I can throw a strike one day like C-C does." N-J happily wraps his arms around Nutsy. "Thank you, Papa."

"Maybe, one day, N-J... maybe one day." As Nutsy's eyes tear up while they hug, he quickly wipes them away before N-J notices because he knows it makes him upset.

This was the hardest decision of Nutsy's life, by far. Yes, the decision with the group is important for his financial security, but having to place his son in a facility doesn't compare to it, one bit. Although Nutsy knows life isn't always fair, it's his son's situation that makes his mind wander about his personal dream.

The next morning, Squalo didn't want to miss the opportunity to find Munchie so he made a bullshit appointment with Munchie's office.

It's now two o'clock in the afternoon and Squalo sits in one of Munchie's patient rooms waiting for him to arrive. Munchie finally enters the room and he exchanges a handshake with Squalo. "Jesus, you must be killing them here," Squalo sarcastically says.

Munchie laughs and replies, "Have you been eating your carrots?"

"Yeah, with some red wine."

Munchie figures he should take this opportunity to ask Squalo about the fix coming up. "So, is there really an under lock coming up?"

What Munchie doesn't realize, is Squalo already has his own plan and agenda for the visit. "Well, that's what I'm here for, Doc."

Munchie appears confused. "For what?"

"I might have a few friends place some bets with your code."

"Nutsy won't allow that."

"I know. You're gonna call it in."

"Come on, Squalo. I can't do —"

Squalo cuts him off. "Yes you can, and you will… just be ready for my call."

"Look, I don't mind helping out, but that's double crossing

Nutsy now."

"She's good, ha?"

"What?"

"How about I let her know you've been spending time with your ex?"

Munchie doesn't respond.

Squalo continues, "Yeah, I thought so. If you can screw over my daughter, I'm sure fucking Nutsy shouldn't be a problem." Squalo turns and walks away.

Munchie's completely caught off guard and remains silent since he and Belinda always try to keep their relationship a secret.

Squalo turns back and says, "I gotta tell you, even though she's a grown woman, she's still my daughter. This ain't sitting right with me."

CHAPTER 18

Later that night, Belinda and Vito are in a heated discussion in her office. Vito has been waiting for her nod to retaliate against either Blackie or Sammy and he's losing his patience.

While she sits at her desk, Belinda slams her fist down and screams, "You're going to wait until I make a final decision! That's it!"

Vito paces back and forth and replies, "Fuck that! It's my name on the line right now."

Belinda hops up from her chair and replies, "I'm the boss, remember that!"

"Yeah, and you're letting them shit all over you. I bet your father would've given the word, that night."

"You stay the hell away from my father. He'll eat you alive."

"At least he has balls."

Belinda gets closer to Vito and replies, "You don't wanna see MY balls, trust me." She tosses a piece of paper at his face. "Now get the fuck out and go do your job!"

Vito squats down, picks up the paper, and storms out of the room.

A few minutes later, Vito and another worker hop in a beat up van in the body shop parking lot. It's Vito's turn to drive tonight so he starts the engine and floors it. The van skids out of the parking lot and flies down a street.

The worker knows Vito's already annoyed from his exchange with Belinda, so he tries to avoid any conversation with him. Vito's the first to speak. "Sometimes, ya just gotta take care of shit on your own terms."

The worker's a faithful employee of Belinda and another member of the Lords. He knows what Vito's underlying message is and tries to put it to bed. "It's not your call. Belinda makes these decisions."

"This is my reputation on the line, not hers."

"Still —"

"Still, nothing! They're gonna both pay when —"

Their next assignment is right ahead, so the man cuts Vito off and yells, "Fucking pay attention, will you! It's the black Lexus ahead on the right. Hit it by the door... now!"

So Vito quickly spins the steering wheel and their van bounces off of the driver's side door of the Lexus and continues down the street. Vito peeks at the rear view mirror and says, "I can't tell. How was that?"

The worker turns and glances out of the back window and replies, "It looks good from here. Belinda will like it. It's probably five grand in damage."

As they continue to drive down the street, the worker peeks at the piece of paper that Belinda had tossed at Vito and says, "Last one. It's a white BMW two blocks over."

While Vito nods, his thoughts drift to his conversation with Squalo. "Ya still bet?"

"Who doesn't in this town?"

"I don't... I need ya to put some bets in for me this weekend."

"Who do you like?"

"It's not for me it's for some of my friends."

"Fuck that. I have a platinum account with Nutsy right now. Set up your own account."

"What's a platinum account?"

"I get a break off the vig because of my payment history."

"What does this guy think he's a credit card company now?"

"Dude, he's bigger than a credit card. Nutsy's the man."

"He ain't shit. I need ya to do this for me. I can't set up an account with him, you know that."

"Oh yeah, I forgot. His daughter fucked you up."

While Vito slams on the brakes and the van skids down the middle of the street, the man lunges forward and smacks his face on the dashboard. "Shit!" The man grabs his nose.

Vito has an irate look and says, "Every big player started somewhere. You'll all fucking see one day... and you're calling in these bets."

Meanwhile, Bono is getting ready to go out for the night. As he walks through the living room in his house, Bono passes a person reading a newspaper in an enclosed porch. The paper is covering the person's face, so it's hard to tell exactly who it is.

While Bono continues to pass by the porch, he accidentally trips over a box on the floor and the person lowers the newspaper. The person is Belo and he says, "Come here a minute."

Bono enters the enclosed porch and replies, "Yeah, Uncle Belo?"

"Where are you going?"

"I'm going out with a friend for a little while."

"I asked you where, not with who."

"I'm going to a bar in The Vern."

"Why there?"

"This girl I know invited me."

"What girl?"

"I met her at a military recruitment center a few months ago."

"Don't make it late like last time, or I'll ship your ass back down south to your father."

That same night, Nutsy and Ladro sit in Nutsy's kitchen at the island, each with a glass of wine in front of them. They are in one of their usual back and forth discussions. Nutsy shakes his head and says, "Will ya stop asking me. Ya can't even squat down right now."

Ladro laughs and replies, "You play golf, right?"

"You know I do, so what?"

"Does it ever rain on the golf course?"

"Where are ya going with this?"

"Just like it never rains to a golfer, a thief's leg never hurts while doing a job." Ladro can't get the safe out of his mind. All he thinks about is what a goldmine it is and this would be a great way to finalize his career. He left right after he got shot and always thought it was never on his own terms.

Nutsy knows this would be suicide for Ladro even though he was a spectacular thief in the past. "You're talkin' about an apple and an orange here."

"Listen, no one ever remembers anyone for being good. You know that, Nutsy. It's only when you're fucking great that you become a legend."

"So now we wanna be legends?"

"Why the fuck not, ha?"

"Maybe Billy's right. We just take the deal and put it to bed."

"And give the extra percentage to the stooges? If you accept now, they'll own you forever... it ain't the Nutsy I know, for sure."

Down deep inside, Nutsy knows Ladro's right but is trying to convince himself otherwise. "The Nutsy you know had more hair on his head too. We all seem to change, don't we?"

"Maybe so, but he also taught me a leopard never changes his spots... you remember that one?"

They stare for a moment in thought. Nutsy has never backed down in the past to anyone. This would surely be a first. He toys with the idea for a moment and then eventually says, "I guess you're either born a lamb or a lion, right?"

"You got that fucking right. But the question is, what are we?"

The last thing Nutsy would ever want to do, is give in to his back-stabbing group. He's torn because he knows between Kathy and Billy, he's going to have hell to pay if he doesn't accept this deal. Ladro stares him straight in the eyes and says, "Just remember, we only need six friends in the end."

As Nutsy stares in thought, his mind drifts to N-J and thinks how simple life must be for him, or maybe, it's just how it appears. All he can envision at this moment is N-J winding up on the mound in front of a large crowd at the sports park and hurling a blazing fastball.

"Nutsy, did I lose you?" Ladro asks when he notices Nutsy drifting away.

Nutsy snaps out of his gaze and replies, "Nah."

"It looked like you were in another world there for a minute."

Nutsy's thoughts now turn toward his group and thinks, how could these guys be such fucking pricks in life and my son never gets the chance to follow his dream? Nutsy's blood boils as his mind continues to roam. Everything I've done for them, all the money I've laid out of my pocket, and never once, did they ever ask about my son.

Ladro says, "Where are you? I think I keep losing you."

Nutsy asks, "You know what this is all about, right?"

"Yeah, they're tryin' to screw us."

"Nah. It's more than that. What happens to lions when they're not hungry anymore?"

"They get soft and lazy, like the ones at the zoo."

"Yeah, I'm not gonna lie. My kids make me think different and the guys know it."

"You're all over the lot now. What are you saying?"

So Nutsy finally raises his glass. "Fuck it. Kathy and Billy ain't gonna be happy, but I guess the stooges just woke the two lions."

Ladro raises his glass and replies, "Now that's the Nutsy I know." Their glasses clink.

Kathy stands on top of the stairs and overhears Nutsy's last comment. Her eyes close as she takes in Nutsy's final decision.

To be continued.

Made in the USA
San Bernardino, CA
01 July 2020